...And Then There Was Nun

by Bruce W. Gilray &
Richard T. Witter

Original Music by
Craig Victor Fenter

A SAMUEL FRENCH ACTING EDITION

SAMUEL FRENCH

FOUNDED 1830

NEW YORK HOLLYWOOD LONDON TORONTO

SAMUELFRENCH.COM

ISBN 978-0-573-69788-3   Printed in U.S.A.   #29261

MUSIC USE NOTE

Licensees are solely responsible for obtaining formal written permission from copyright owners to use copyrighted music in the performance of this play and are strongly cautioned to do so. If no such permission is obtained by the licensee, then the licensee must use only original music that the licensee owns and controls. Licensees are solely responsible and liable for all music clearances and shall indemnify the copyright owners of the play and their licensing agent, Samuel French, Inc., against any costs, expenses, losses and liabilities arising from the use of music by licensees.

IMPORTANT BILLING AND CREDIT
REQUIREMENTS

All producers of ...*AND THEN THERE WAS NUN must* give credit to the Author of the Play in all programs distributed in connection with performances of the Play, and in all instances in which the title of the Play appears for the purposes of advertising, publicizing or otherwise exploiting the Play and/or a production. The name of the Author *must* appear on a separate line on which no other name appears, immediately following the title and *must* appear in size of type not less than fifty percent of the size of the title type.

In addition the following credit must be given in all programs and publicity information distributed in association with this piece:

...AND THEN THERE WAS NUN (100%)
Written by Bruce W. Gilray & Richard T. Witter (50%)
Original Music by Craig Victor Fenter (40%)

*... **AND THEN THERE WAS NUN*** was produced in 1990, 1991 and 1992 by Toto Too Productions (Producers: Bruce W. Gilray, Susan A. Lyon and Richard T. Witter) at the St. Genesius Theatre in West Hollywood, CA. The play was directed by Bruce W. Gilray. The Stage Manager and Set Designer was Susan A. Lyon. The Assistant Stage Managers were Darren L. Isabelle, Sandy Bellevue. The Choreographer was Darren L. Isabelle. The Lighting Designers were F. Thom Spadaro, Mike Salinas, Buddy Tobie. The Sound Designers were Kirkanthony Bernard, F. Thom Spadaro. The Costumers were Pershing Powell, Belvia Isabelle, Francesca Peppiatt. The Technical Director was Richard Lintz. The Hair Stylists were Kirkanthony Bernard and Jonathan Wells. The casts were as follows:

SISTER ALFRED: . . . . Jonathan Wells, Steven Wayne-Fisher, Andy Powell

SISTER HATTIE: . . . . Bill E. Hall

SISTER VIVIEN: . . . . Judy Young

SISTER JOAN: . . . . Annella Keys, Michael Latsch

SISTER BETTE: . . . . Muzzy Lambert, Michael Gerard

SISTER GLORIA: . . . . Francesca Peppiatt, Monica Horan

SISTER TALLULAH: . . . . George Cain

SISTER KATHARINE: . . . . Tif Rice, Lori Thimsen

SISTER MAE: . . . . Jorli McLain, Julia McDowell, Susan A. Lyon, Victoria Mills

SISTER JUDY: . . . . Kimberly Alexander, Wendy Miklovic

SISTER MARILYN: . . . . Elliot Rogers, Maureen Joyce, Elissa Negrin, Julia McDowell

*... **AND THEN THERE WAS NUN*** was produced in 1993, 1996, 2000 and 2004 by the Palos Verdes Players in Torrance, CA. The Directors were Tony Torrisi and F. Thom Spadaro. The Producer was Susan A. Lyon. The Composer was Craig Victor Fenter. The Choreographers were Darren L. Isabelle, Ray Odell, Susan A. Lyon. The Stage Managers were Jennifer Roberts, Mike Cullen, Diana Mann. The Set Designers were Maxine Whittaker, Susan A. Lyon, Sam Uskovich. The Construction Foreman was Gary Krenz. The Scenic Artists were Helen Fearon, Mary Ann Drake, Daryl Hogue, Rita Hull, Pat Moriarty, Sam Uskovich, Vera Zuckett. The Set Decorator/Properties Mistress was Susan A. Lyon. The Light Designers were Jennifer Roberts, Dan Weingarten, Buddy Tobie. The Sound Designers were Ken Sekiguchi, F. Thom Spadaro. The Costumers were Louise Battey, Kathy Martin, Susan Tucker, Diana Mann. The casts were as follows:

SISTER ALFRED: . . . . Ramsey Warfield, Jesse Schoem, Susan "Sam" Jones, Frank Thomas

SISTER HATTIE: . . . . Keith D. Robinson, Michael William James, Rodney Riley, Daniel A. Tennant

SISTER VIVIEN: . . . . Mina Dillard, Alexandra Hoover, Terri Lynn Harris, Oriana Nicole Tavoularis

SISTER JOAN: . . . . Douglas Jacobs, Martha Duncan, Michael Latsch

SISTER BETTE: . . . . . . Robin McWilliams, Shelley Werk, Michael Latsch, Michael Anthony Nozzi

SISTER TALLULAH: . . . . Tyrie McCulley, Geraldine D. Fuentes

SISTER GLORIA: . . . . Laura Pursell, Liza Hayes, Lauren Fleishman, Suki Lammers

SISTER KATHARINE: . . . . Dani Ballew, Angela Hoover, K.B. Dulude, Margaret Schugt

SISTER MAE: . . . . Doreen Zetterlund, Martha Duncan, Diane O'Neill, Kari Hefner

SISTER JUDY: . . . . Natanya Rose, Heather Ryon

SISTER MARILYN: . . . . Kathleen Spillane, Averie Maddox, Kim Mellman, Martha Duncan

CHARACTERS
(In order of appearance)

SISTER ALFRED – Similar to Alfred Hitchcock in both voice and stature. He is the narrator. He wears a black suit, white shirt, thin black tie and a black-and-white nun's wimple.

SISTER HATTIE – Similar to Mammy in *Gone With The Wind*. She is the housekeeper at the retreat. While loyal to Sister Vivien, she definitely has a mind of her own. She is attired in a full-length black skirt, white shirt and full-length white apron. A black-and-white bandana and nun's wimple adorn her head. She wears a full-length red petticoat under her black skirt.

SISTER VIVIEN – Similar to Scarlett O'Hara in *Gone With The Wind*. She is the ambitious, calculating, conceited social director. A woman who will stop at nothing to become the head of the Order. She is attired in a black-and-white hoop dress and a black-and-white nun's wimple and wears a ring mirror on her finger and carries a fan.

SISTER JOAN – Similar to Blanche Hudson in *Whatever Happened To Baby Jane?* She is the invalid sister of Sister Bette. She is attired in a black evening gown with padded shoulders. She wears black spike heels with ankle straps. On top of a 40's style hairdo is a black-and-white nun's wimple. She spends most of the play in a wheelchair.

SISTER BETTE – Similar to Baby Jane Hudson in *Whatever Happened To Baby Jane?* She is a middle-aged, demented woman who mentally tortures her invalid sister, Sister Joan. She is attired in a white, old-fashioned child's dress, black-and-white striped stockings and black Mary Jane shoes. Her blond curls hang out from under a black-and-white nun's wimple. Her make-up is of a white, grotesque type.

SISTER GLORIA – Similar to Norma Desmond in *Sunset Boulevard*. She is an aged, spaced-out, silent film star. Though coherent, she generally lives in her own world. She is attired in a 50's style flared-leg pantsuit/skirt. She wears heavy makeup. She wears a turban with a large feather and a black-and-white nun's wimple. One curl peeks out under the turban on her forehead. She frequently uses a finger-held cigarette holder.

SISTER TALLULAH – Similar to Tallulah Bankhead in every movie she ever made. She is freewheeling, hard-drinking and outspoken. She is attired in a satin, tea-length evening gown. She wears a black-and-white wimple over her wavy, shoulder-length auburn hair.

SISTER KATHARINE – Similar to Ethel Thayer in *On Golden Pond*. She is a tough, seasoned and determined woman. Her speech is tremored. She is attired in a black pantsuit with a white turtleneck shirt. She wears a black-and-white wimple, upon which a bun covered in a hairnet is attached. The headdress resembles Queen Eleanor in *The Lion in Winter*.

SISTER MAE – Similar to Lady Lou in *She Done Him Wrong*. She is a sultry, wisecracking woman of ample endowment. She is attired in a black-and-white form-fitting sequined evening gown with matching feather boa. On top of her bleached blonde hair is a black-and-white nun's wimple. At the beginning of the play, she wears an oversized hat.

SISTER JUDY – Similar to Dorothy Gale in *The Wizard of Oz*. She is a young, innocent, bubbly girl from Kansas. She carries a mechanical toy dog that barks on command and with whom she converses. She is attired in a checkered, black-and-white farm girl-type dress. (This will change once during the play to a matching dress in blue-and-white checks). She wears white bobby socks and black pumps. (She will change to blue bobby socks and red ruby shoes during the play). Her long auburn hair is in braids with bows matching her dress and a black-and-white nun's wimple.

SISTER MARILYN – Similar to Sugar Kane in *Some Like It Hot*. She is a voluptuous, dumb-blonde-type who thinks the best of everyone. She is attired in a 50's style flowing, white pleated dress. She wears matching spiked heels. Her blonde hair is adorned by a black-and-white nun's wimple.

ACT I

Scene One: Friday afternoon and evening

ACT II

Scene One: Saturday morning
Scene Two: Later that evening
Scene Three: Sunday morning

SETTING

The entire action of the play takes place in the living room of a mansion on *Grauman's Chinese Island*. It is a lavish, Art Deco interior painted and furnished entirely in black and white. Upstage center is the main entrance to the room that leads off to the front entranceway. Offstage is the front door. A replica of the Grauman's Chinese Theater pillars frames the entranceway. On the wall, next to the stage left pillar, is a mounted iPod. The walls of the room are covered with handprints, footprints and signatures of famous movie stars. There is a balcony running from a closet at stage right to a large picture window at stage left with floor-length drapes that can be opened and closed. The floor of the balcony and entranceway is done in black and white checkered tiles. Outside the window stands a large tree with one horizontal limb visible through the window. A curtain hangs on a rod that covers the closet. The curtain can be entirely opened and closed. To the upstage left of the closet is a pedestal with a small gold statue. At the center of the balcony are three wide steps that descend to the main floor. To the left of the stairs is a large planter with a black-and-white miniature palm tree that can be uprooted. Downstage right, and prominently displayed, is a tall pedestal on top of which is a ring of (10) 6" china nuns and a portrait of "Mother Paramount," hanging on the wall above the china nun ring. In the portrait, she is wearing a veil, which obscures her face. The portrait is hinged to the wall so that it can be opened and closed from backstage. Upstage of the portrait is a small table with a coffee service. Upstage of the coffee service is a hallway entrance that leads off stage right to the kitchen. Upstage left is a Victrola. Down stage of the Victrola is a hallway that leads off stage left to the bedrooms. Down stage of the hallway is a hidden passage behind an 8' tall gold statue. There are light switch plates next to all three (3) entranceways. In the mid-stage left area is a love seat sofa and behind it is a sofa table on which there is a telephone. In the mid-stage right area is a bar and two bar stools with easy access around and behind. Behind the bar is a shelf unit on which are numerous items including a prominently displayed framed poem entitled, "Ten Sisters of San Andreas."

Ten Sisters of San Andreas

*   *Ten Sisters of San Andreas playing with a vine,*
      One went and hung herself, and then there were nine.

*   *Nine Sisters of San Andreas all playing with fate,*
      One went for bust, and then there were eight.

*   *Eight Sisters of San Andreas aiming for heaven,*
      One became a centerfold, and then there were seven.

*   *Seven Sisters of San Andreas acting in the flicks,*
      One's career got cut, and then there were six.

*   *Six Sisters of San Andreas playing near a hive,*
      One got stung, and then there were five.

*   *Five Sisters of San Andreas finding one a bore,*
      They locked her in the closet, and then there were four.

*   *Four Sisters of San Andreas amid a murderer's spree,*
      One's chalice was poisoned, and then there were three.

*   *Three Sisters of San Andreas discovering a clue,*
      It played heavy on one's mind, and then there were two.

*   *Two Sisters of San Andreas playing with a gun,*
      One got herself shot, and then there was one.

*   *One Sister of San Andreas thinking she'd won,*
      A red herring deceived her…

…AND THEN THERE WAS NUN.

Prologue

*(Stage is black. Opening music is **Sister Alfred's Theme**.)*

(As the lights come up, a 4' x 8' sign is revealed. On it is the outline of a well recognized caricature in profile. Next to the caricature is a simple map marked with the letters "A" and "B." Point "A" indicates the "Bates Motel;" Point "B" indicates "Grauman's Chinese Theatre." At the top of the map is a detailed drawing of the "HOLLYWOOD" sign marked as Point "C." The second "L" in the word "HOLLYWOOD" is detachable, so that when it is removed, the word then reads "HOLYWOOD." Also prominently displayed on the sign are the compass points "N-E-W-S." We see the legs and feet of a tech person who is holding the sign from behind.)

*(From stage right enters a rather portly nun who bears a striking resemblance to Alfred Hitchcock. A spot light illuminates him as he moves slowly across the stage ending center stage. Once he lines up with the profile drawn on the sign, he pauses and turns to the audience. After **Sister Alfred's Theme** ends, he delivers his monologue. Emphasis is given to all the bolded references.)*

ALFRED. Good evening, ladies and gentlemen, and welcome to our show. I am your host for this evening, Sister Alfred. Tonight's story takes place on the eve of the annual retreat of the Holy Order of Our Sisters of San Andreas; an order founded one night by a young starlet named **Rebecca**, who lived at the **Bates Motel** referred to on our map as Point "A."

(He indicates Point "A" on the map with a pointer.)

ALFRED. *(cont.)* One night, while attending a premiere at Grauman's Chinese Theater, Point "B"...

(He indicates Point "B" on the map with a pointer.)

...she looked through her limousine's **Rear Window** and spotted a **Notorious** young lad named **Norman** who held her **Spellbound**. He persuaded her to join him for a picnic lunch beneath the "Hollywood" sign, Point "C."

(He indicates Point "C" on the map with a pointer.)

They traveled **North by Northwest** until they reached the mountain. Although she suffered from **Vertigo**, they climbed the **Thirty-Nine Steps** through a large flock of **Birds** to the base of the second "L." Suddenly, he lunged at her with a lust-driven **Frenzy**, ripping her clothes and breaking her **Topaz** necklace. She realized beyond a **Shadow of a Doubt** that she must escape from this perverted **Psycho** or she would be up a creek without a **Lifeboat**. Then fate intervened. At that precise moment an earthquake, measuring 7.2 on Mr. Richter's scale, hit the San Andreas Fault. She was thrown free from her attacker who was struck down by the third consonant of the crumbling "Hollywood" sign.

(He reaches up to the map and removes the second "L" in "HOLLYWOOD.")

(pause) He got the "L" knocked out of him. *(laughs dryly)* Ha. Ha...Ha. To little Rebecca this was a sign from God. He had blessed her and saved her. He had delivered her from evil for a purpose. She cast her eyes skyward and saw the sign He had given her; and that sign said *"Holy-wood."* She knew the Lord had chosen her to found an Order and she called that order "The Sisters of San Andreas on

Sunset Boulevard." It would be devoted to God, stars, premieres, and the cinema magic we call "Movies."

*(**Sister Alfred's Theme** begins to play. **ALFRED** exits stage right, followed by the tech person carrying the sign.)*

(Blackout)

*(**Sister Alfred's Theme** continues to play to end.)*

ACT I

Scene One

(As the lights fade up, the interior of the living room of a mansion is revealed. **SISTER HATTIE** *is on the balcony looking out through the window curtains. She is carrying a feather duster. Centerstage and looking toward the audience at an imaginary "fourth wall" mirror is* **SISTER VIVIEN**. *She is checking her make-up, as she should do whenever she can throughout the play. She also frequently checks her lipstick in the reflection of a jeweled mirror ring she wears on her finger. A **steam boat whistle** is heard.)*

HATTIE. *(excitedly)* The Sisters are coming! The Sisters are coming! The boat's a comin' in to the dock!

*(**HATTIE** descends stairs and crosses to **VIVIEN**.)*

That means we're gonna be up to our armpits in white folks any minute! What are we gonna do? What are we gonna say? Tell me why I should give a damn!

VIVIEN. Oh, fiddle-dee-dee, Sister Hattie. Calm down. We still have a few minutes before this years participants arrive.

*(**VIVIEN** adjusts her cleavage and looks at her reflection in the "mirror.")*

(to herself)

I shouldn't tamper with perfection.

15

(**VIVIEN** *gives two "air kisses" to her reflection.*)

HATTIE. Well I would…and I done told you and I done told you, it ain't fit and proper for a lady to show her bosom before three o'clock.

(**HATTIE** *adjusts* **VIVIEN**'s *dress.*)

VIVIEN. (*to* **HATTIE**, *threateningly*) You just make sure you got your act together, Sister. I don't want anything to go wrong with this retreat. If I pull this off I'm sure to become something more than a common social director. Maybe, someday…Supreme Commander of our Order.

(*egotistically*)

Mother Vivien, the First. Nothing will stop me! Do you hear? Nothing!

(*indicates portrait of "Mother Paramount"*)

Not even our foundress, Mother Paramount!

(**HATTIE** *dusts the portrait with the feather duster.*)

HATTIE. Mmm-mmm-mmm. She certainly is a mystery, isn't she child?

VIVIEN. Never seen…never heard from…always in the shadows…never knowing exactly what she does, and most people don't even know that she exists.

HATTIE. It's sorta like being Vice President, ain't it?

(*A **gong doorbell** is heard.*)

(**VIVIEN** *and* **HATTIE** *excitedly rush towards the stairs to greet their guests; bumping into each other.*)

VIVIEN. Get those colored lights going!

HATTIE. Colored? You watch your mouth, Little Missy…

(**HATTIE** *crosses behind the sofa to retrieve two flashlights that resemble those used by airline workers to "park" an airplane. She leaves the feather duster on the bottom shelf of the sofa table.* **VIVIEN** *turns on* *the iPod. We hear sounds of **applause and crowd cheering.** VIVIEN pulls a cell phone from her bodice and exits out the entranceway to open the front door offstage. She backs into the room taking video of her guests with the cell phone as they enter. Behind her, **HATTIE** waves the two flashlights like klieg lights at a movie premiere.)*

*(**SISTER BETTE** enters pushing **SISTER JOAN**, who is in a wheelchair. **BETTE** and **JOAN** remove their sunglasses and pose as **VIVIEN** takes their picture with the cell phone.)*

(They perform a ritual two-cheek "air-kiss.")

ALL. Let's do lunch!

*(**VIVIEN** puts the cell phone back in her bodice.)*

VIVIEN. Welcome, Sisters Bette and Joan, to the Sisters of San Andreas' annual retreat. Sister Hattie and I have finished all the preparations for the weekend.

*(As **VIVIEN** speaks, **BETTE** exits briefly and tosses one black and one white suitcase through the front entranceway, not caring where they land or what they hit.)*

JOAN. Don't forget my precious, little Pookie.

*(**BETTE** re-enters with a birdcage with a fake bird in it.)*

Come on, sister, give me the bird.

*(**BETTE** does a double-take to the audience.)*

BETTE. With pleasure, sister dear.

*(**BETTE** drops the birdcage in **JOAN**'s lap and begins pacing the balcony.)*

(perturbed) Well...will you take a look at this place? Mother Paramount expects us to stay in this Art Deco nightmare? Ha! What a dump!

JOAN. Please, Bette, remember you're a guest. I'm sure that by tomorrow everything will look better.

(*looks smugly at* **VIVIEN**)

After all, tomorrow is another day.

VIVIEN. (*sarcastically*) Yes...well...I'll have to remember that.

BETTE. (*indicating Vivien's dress*) By the way, Sister Vivien, may I say that your dress makes such lovely drapes...er...um...I mean...drapes so well.

VIVIEN. (*catty*) Yes, well...may I say, Sister Bette, what semi-tasteful gloves you have on?

(**BETTE** *admires her black-and-white spotted gloves.*)

BETTE. Yah, Mr. Disney asked me to watch his puppies for the weekend!

JOAN. I'll have to apologize for my sister, Sisters. I don't know what's gotten into her lately. The doctors say that she's showing signs of a neurotic and depraved personality. Quite possibly even with homicidal tendencies.

(*aside to* **VIVIEN**)

But I think she's just trying to get on *"Jerry Springer."*

BETTE. What d'ya mean, neurotic? You're the one who's neurotic. I don't know where you get your ideas, sister.

(*pause*)

Fasten your seat belt; it's going to be a bumpy flight.

(*While holding onto the handles,* **BETTE** *pushes* **JOAN**'s *wheelchair roughly down the stairs ending center stage*)

JOAN. (*regaining composure*) Oh, sister! You wouldn't be able to do that if I wasn't in this wheelchair.

BETTE. *(knowingly to audience)* But ya are, sister…

> (**BETTE** *shoves the wheelchair sideways with her foot.*)

…ya are in a wheelchair!

VIVIEN. *(apprehensively)* I…I…I'm sure you'll find your quarters quite comfortable. Sister Hattie, show them to their rooms.

> (*The* **gong doorbell** *is heard.*)

> (**HATTIE** *picks up their suitcases and exits out bedroom hallway, followed by* **BETTE** *and* **JOAN.**)

> (**VIVIEN** *turns on the iPod. Sounds of* **applause and crowd cheering.** **VIVIEN** *again pulls the cell phone from her bodice and exits out the entranceway to open the front door offstage. She backs into the room taking video of her guests with the cell phone.*)

> (**SISTER TALLULAH** *and* **SISTER GLORIA** *enter.* **GLORIA** *carries a large black suitcase.* **TALLULAH** *is carrying a black portable bar with the word* **"BAR"** *prominently labeled on one side.*)

> (**GLORIA** *and* **TALLULAH** *remove their sunglasses and pose as* **VIVIEN** *takes their picture with the cell phone. They perform the ritual two-cheek "air-kiss."*)

ALL. Let's do lunch!

> (**VIVIEN** *puts the cell phone back in her bodice.*)

VIVIEN. *(greeting the sisters)* Sister Tallulah, Sister Gloria, welcome to our annual retreat. Sister Hattie will be back presently to show you to your rooms and then you can meet the others. Sister Tallulah, just leave your luggage up here.

> (**VIVIEN** *tries to take* **TALLULAH**'s *portable bar, but* **TALLULAH** *pulls it away indignantly, revealing the word* **"BAR"** *to the audience.*)

TALLULAH. I don't think so, dahling.

VIVIEN. Okay…make yourselves at home.

(*to* **GLORIA**)

May I take your coat?

GLORIA. Thank you.

(**GLORIA** *drops her coat on the floor and descends the stairs dramatically. A bewildered* **VIVIEN** *picks up the coat and hangs it up in the closet.*)

Don't worry. I'll meet everyone. All my adoring fans…the press…you know, the little people. But I can't…I can't…I'm not ready to meet my public now.

(**GLORIA** *crosses to the sofa, reclines like Cleopatra and lights a cigarette in a finger-held holder.*)

TALLULAH. You must try to forgive Sister Gloria, dahling. She's been this way ever since her monkey died.

(**TALLULAH** *descends stairs and crosses behind the bar.*)

Now, with whom do you have to copulate to get a drink around here?

(*surveys room*)

Black and white, black and white, black and white. Oh, I just love this black and white decor. Obviously the landlord isn't Ted Turner. (*laughs*) By the way, where is Mother Paramount anyhow?

VIVIEN. I'm afraid that Mother Paramount has been detained until later.

(*The* **gong doorbell** *is heard again.*)

(**VIVIEN** *turns on the iPod. Sounds of* **applause and crowd cheering**. **VIVIEN** *again pulls the cell phone from her bodice and exits out the entranceway to open the front door offstage. She backs into the room taking video of her guests with the cell phone.*)

(**SISTER KATHARINE** *enters carrying a carpet bag suitcase followed by* **SISTER MAE** *carrying a large black suitcase with a cursive letter "M" prominently painted on one side.* **MAE** *is wearing an extremely oversized, feathered hat.*)

(**KATHARINE** *and* **MAE** *remove their sunglasses and pose as* **VIVIEN** *takes their picture with the cell phone. They perform the ritual two-cheek "air-kiss."*)

ALL. Let's do lunch!

(**VIVIEN** *puts the cell phone back in her bodice.*)

KATHARINE. How do you do? I'm Sister Katharine and this is Sister Mae. Sister Streisand would have come with us, but we couldn't fit her ego on the boat.

(*to* **VIVIEN**)

Are you Mother Paramount?

TALLULAH. (*interrupting* **VIVIEN**) No, dahling. The Big Mother is stuck somewhere and won't be charming us with her presence until later.

VIVIEN. (*responding to* **KATHARINE**) I'm Sister Vivien, your activities director.

MAE. Oh, honey. Where I come from we'd call you a pimp.

VIVIEN. (*ignoring* **MAE**) Let me introduce you to the others. On the couch we have Sister Gloria and holding up the bar is Sister Tallulah.

TALLULAH. Sister Mae and I already know each other, dahling.

MAE. Oh, Sister Tallulah has been around these parts for over forty years. Of course, her face has been around considerably longer.

TALLULAH. Yes, dahling, I met Mae when the Earth was still cooling.

(*to* **MAE**)

TALLULAH. *(cont.)* As always, an *endurance* to see you again. Why don't you come on down here and have yourself a little drink.

(**MAE** *descends stairs to bar.*)

MAE. Don't mind if I do.

TALLULAH. As you can see, we're well stocked...much like your hips.

(**MAE** *sits on the stage left barstool.*)

MAE. I think I'll rearrange your teeth.

(**MAE** *holds out her hand.*)

Why don't you toss 'em over?

VIVIEN. May I say, Sister Katharine, what a most attractive wrap you have.

KATHARINE. Thank you. It was a gift from Sister Elizabeth Taylor...Hilton-Wilding...Todd-Fisher...Burton-Burton...Warner-Fortensky...Taylor. She gave it to me, *suddenly last summer.*

VIVIEN. Is it imported velvet?

KATHARINE. No, domestic.

VIVIEN. *(disappointedly)* Oh...*national velvet.*

(**KATHARINE** *descends the stairs and surveys the room.*)

KATHARINE. Why, this place is just marvelous. Oh, Mae, I think we're going to have a lovely time here this weekend. Peace and quiet...

(motioning around room)

...surrounded by all these quaint an...

(to **GLORIA***)*

...*tiques.*

(back to the other Sisters)

This reminds me of the home I had in Philadelphia. Did I ever tell you about the time I lived in Philadelphia?

TALLULAH. *(interrupting)* Spare us the trite details, dahling. This is one inquiring mind that doesn't want to know.

KATHARINE. Really Sister Tallulah! Such rudeness! I'd wish you'd remember that you are a member of the Sisters of San Andreas.

*(**GLORIA** begins to imitate **KATHARINE**'s headshaking mannerisms.)*

We are an order of dedicated individuals brought together by our leader, Mother Paramount, to further the moral code of the Hays Office. We perform our vocation by emulating the goddesses of the cinema. As an Order, it is our function, nay...

*(**GLORIA**'s headshaking becomes uncontrollable and she falls off the sofa and onto the floor. **KATHARINE** turns and glares at **GLORIA**, who, regaining her dignity, climbs back onto sofa and reclines.)*

...our duty, to guide others,

*(indicating **GLORIA**)*

no matter how *annoying* they may be, to accept, as divine spirituality, the silver screen!

*(All applaud enthusiastically, except **TALLULAH** who claps slowly and sarcastically. **HATTIE** enters from bedroom hallway, crosses to the stairs.)*

VIVIEN. *(eager to break the tension)* Oh, Sister Hattie, I'd like you to meet our other guests.

KATHARINE. How do you do? I'm Sister Katharine.

HATTIE. *(to **KATHARINE**)* Sister.

KATHARINE. *(to **HATTIE**)* Sister.

*(introduces **MAE** to **HATTIE**)*

And this is Sister Mae.

MAE. Oh, Sister.

HATTIE. *(mimicking Mae)* Oh, Sister.

(*VIVIEN admonishes* **HATTIE**.)

TALLULAH. Sister Hattie, why don't you be a dahling and take the *bags* to their rooms. Oh, and don't forget the *luggage*.

(**HATTIE** *picks up the suitcases and leads* **KATHA-RINE** *and* **MAE** *toward the bedroom hallway.*)

KATHARINE. Come along Mae. I don't know about you, but I'd rather be stuck in some roach-infested motel then spend another minute with her.

(*indicating* **TALLULAH**)

GLORIA. I was once in a roach motel. I checked in... but I never checked out.

(*The* **gong doorbell** *is heard again.*)

(**KATHARINE** *throws her hands up in dismay as she and* **MAE** *follow* **HATTIE** *out to the bedroom hall-way.*)

(**VIVIEN** *turns on the iPod. Sounds of* **applause and crowd cheering**. **VIVIEN** *pulls the cell phone from her bodice and exits out the entranceway to open the front door offstage. She again backs into the room taking video of her guests with the cell phone.*)

(**SISTER MARILYN** *and* **SISTER JUDY** *enter.* **MARI-LYN** *carries a white vanity case and a small white purse with reading glasses inside.* **JUDY** *carries a white basket, a large bottle of pills and Toto, a mechanical dog, who wears a collar, leash and sun-glasses. They are gazing around the room ignoring* **VIVIEN**.)

VIVIEN. (*aside to* **TALLULAH**) Look who's here...the *simple* Sisters.

(*to* **MARILYN** *and* **JUDY** [*trying to get their atten-tion*])

Yoo-hoo!

(**MARILYN** *and* **JUDY** *remove their sunglasses and pose as* **VIVIEN** *takes their picture with the cell phone. They perform the ritual two-cheek "air-kiss."*)

MARILYN & JUDY.	**VIVIEN, TALLULAH & GLORIA.**
(in unison, loud and proudly)	*(in unison)*
Let's do *breakfast!*	Let's do lunch!

(**VIVIEN** *and* **TALLULAH** *exchange glances and shake their heads incredulously.* **VIVIEN** *puts the cell phone back in her bodice.*)

VIVIEN. Welcome Sisters.

> (*to* **JUDY & MARILYN**, *as explaining to a child*)
>
> I – am – your – co – or – di – na – tor. Sis – ter – Viv – i – en

JUDY. Well, hello. I'm Sister Judy and this is my dog, Toto. We go everywhere together. Well, say hello, Toto.

TOTO. Bark, bark, bark, bark.

JUDY. Toto says he's very pleased to make your acquaintance. And, this is Sister Marilyn.

MARILYN. *(curtsying)* A pleasure, I'm sure, to meet me. Is Mother Paramount here? I'd be just *dilated* to meet her.

JUDY. No, no, that's *delighted*, Sister Marilyn, *delighted* to meet you.

(**MARILYN** *shakes* **JUDY**'*s hand.*)

MARILYN. Delighted to meet you, too. But don't I already know you?

(**JUDY** *pulls away and hugs* **TOTO**.)

JUDY. Oh my! People come and go so quickly here.

(**JUDY** *pops a pill into her mouth.*)

Or is it just me?

VIVIEN. I'm a...

(**TALLULAH** *overlaps dialogue.*)

VIVIEN & TALLULAH. *(very quickly)* ...fraid that Mother Paramount has been detained.

> *(**BETTE** pushes **JOAN** onstage forcefully propelling the wheelchair into the sofa, startling **GLORIA**.)*

VIVIEN. Here, let me introduce you to the other guests.

> *(**VIVIEN**, **JUDY**, and **MARILYN** descend stairs and meet **BETTE** and **JOAN**.)*

Sisters Marilyn and Judy, may I present Sisters Bette and Joan?

> *(**JUDY** and **MARILYN** walk to each Sister as they greet each of them, much like a wedding reception. The other Sisters remain in their spots.)*

JUDY. *(nodding her head to **JOAN**)* Sister.

JOAN. *(nodding her head to **JUDY**)* Sister.

> *(As **JUDY** greets **BETTE**, **MARILYN** simultaneously greets **JOAN**. **MARILYN** follows **JUDY** as they continue 'greeting' the Sisters. Their dialogue overlaps.)*

JUDY. *(nodding her head to **BETTE**)* Sister	**MARILYN.** *(nodding her head to **JOAN**)* Sister
BETTE. *(nodding her head to **JUDY**)* Sister	**JOAN.** *(nodding her head to **MARILYN**)* Sister
JUDY. *(nodding her head to **VIVIEN**)* Sister	**MARILYN.** *(nodding her head to **BETTE**)* Sister
VIVIEN. *(nodding her head to **JUDY**)* Sister	**BETTE.** *(nodding her head to **MARILYN**)* Sister
*(**JUDY** returns to the place where she began her greetings and watches **MARILYN** as she finishes greeting **VIVIEN**.)*	**MARILYN.** *(nodding her head to **VIVIEN**)* Sister
	VIVIEN. *(nodding her head to **MARILYN**)* Sister

VIVIEN. *(gesturing towards **TALLULAH**, who crosses next to **JOAN**)*

Tending bar this weekend, Sister Tallulah.

JUDY. *(nodding her head to* **TALLULAH***)* Sister.

TALLULAH. *(nodding her head to* **JUDY***)* Sister.

(As **JUDY** *greets* **JOAN**, **MARILYN** *simultaneously greets* **TALLULAH**. **MARILYN** *follows* **JUDY** *as they continue to greet the Sisters, again.)*

JUDY. *(nodding her head to* **JOAN***)* Sister

MARILYN. *(nodding her head to* **TALLULAH***)* Sister

JOAN. *(nodding her head to* **JUDY***)* Sister

TALLULAH. *(nodding her head to* **MARILYN***)* Sister

JUDY. *(nodding her head to* **BETTE***)* Sister

MARILYN. *(nodding her head to* **JOAN***)* Sister

BETTE. *(nodding her head to* **JUDY***)* Sister

JOAN. *(nodding her head to* **MARILYN***)* Sister

JUDY. *(nodding her head to* **VIVIEN***)* Sister

MARILYN. *(nodding her head to* **BETTE***)* Sister

VIVIEN. *(nodding her head to* **JUDY***)* Sister

BETTE. *(nodding her head to* **MARILYN***)* Sister

*(***JUDY** *returns to the place where she began her greetings and watches* **MARILYN** *as she finishes Greeting* **VIVIEN**. *The other sisters exchange looks of "what's going on here?"*

MARILYN. *(nodding her head to* **VIVIEN***)* Sister

VIVIEN. *(nodding her head to* **MARILYN***)* Sister

VIVIEN. *(interrupting)* And currently on leave from Bellevue, Sister Gloria.

(Before **JUDY** *and* **MARILYN** *have a chance to repeat the greeting ceremony once again,* **GLORIA** *rises off the sofa, wearing a false moustache, and passes exaggeratedly through the group.)*

GLORIA. How do you do?

*(***GLORIA** *exits to the kitchen hallway, ala Charlie Chaplin.)*

(The other Sisters look at each other in astonishment.)

JUDY, MARILYN, BETTE & JOAN. *(cautiously)* Sister?

TALLULAH. Can we stop with all this "sister" crap? I'm developing a lisp.

*(**TALLULAH** crosses back to behind the bar.)*

VIVIEN. Don't forget, y'all. Our opening ceremony rehearsal commences in just a short while.

*(to **MARILYN** and **JUDY**)*

Come, you two, I'll show you to your rooms.

*(**VIVIEN** checks her make-up in the "fourth wall" mirror as she exits to bedroom hallway. **MARILYN** also checks her make-up in the "mirror" before exiting.)*

MARILYN. That sounds great to me. I'd like to make myself a little fresh.

*(**VIVIEN**, **JUDY** and **MARILYN** exit to bedroom hallway.)*

TALLULAH. If she were any fresher, we'd have to harvest her.

BETTE. *(laughing)* Oh Tallulah, you little fox.

*(**BETTE** shoves **JOAN**'s wheelchair into the stairs then crosses to stage right barstool and sits.)*

TALLULAH. Yes dahling. Why don't you have a little drink?

*(Perturbed at having being shoved into the stairs, **JOAN** spins her chair around and wheels to the stage left side of the bar. Once settled, **JOAN** reaches into her purse and produces a mirror with her likeness on the back. She checks her hair and lipstick.)*

BETTE. Don't mind if I do. 7-up...

(TALLULAH checks the bar for ingredients for BET-TE's drink.)

TALLULAH. *(repeating)* 7-up…

BETTE. Grenadine…

TALLULAH. *(repeating)* Grenadine…

BETTE. and Kahlua.

TALLULAH. *(repeating)* and Kahlua…

(realizing)

Ah, dahling, a Shirley Temple Black.

(laughs)

(TALLULAH hands BETTE her drink.)

(to JOAN, dryly)

And what'll you have?

JOAN. *(perturbed)* I'll have a Pepsi.

(TALLULAH hands JOAN a bottle of Pepsi who poses with it briefly as in a commercial.)

TALLULAH. *(getting exasperated waiting for JOAN to stop posing)* Well…

(They all raise their drinks together.)

ALL. HOORAY FOR HOLYWOOD!

(JOAN unsuccessfully tries to pry open the sealed bottle of Pepsi with her bare hands, then on the side of her wheelchair and finally with her teeth. Ultimately giving up, she poses with the bottle again.)

TALLULAH. So tell me, fellow Sisters, how did you end up in this holy asylum?

JOAN. I really have no idea. Quite possibly, Mother Paramount thought our work with young children was beneficial and deserved recognition. You see, Sister Bette, here, is the director of the "Whip-In-Hand Correctional Institute" and I'm the child guidance counselor. And how about yourself?

TALLULAH. For the past five years, I've been the chairman of the order's AA program. I drank my way to the top of the bottom of the heap...It was the most horrendous...

JOAN. Big deal! You want gut-wrenching tragedy...

(**BETTE** *rises and begins to pace the floor.*)

BETTE....Oh, Joan, you're not going to bring up that night on *Flamingo Road* are ya?

JOAN. Why shouldn't she know? Why shouldn't everybody know what you did to me?

TALLULAH. My Gawd, this sounds better than an episode of *"Dr. Phil!"* What's this all about?

BETTE. It's about Joan and my ex-husband. Years ago I received a phone call from a stranger. Her name was *Eve*. Eve, Eve, "little Miss Evil." She told me that she saw my dear, sweet, loyal, *tramp* of a sister leaving a hotel with my husband. Well, I decided to confront her that evening. I suggested we go out for a little drive. We borrowed Jane's Hudson.

JOAN. No, dear, it was Mildred's Pierce.

BETTE. *(agitatedly)* Whatever! It was a car! We were crossing a bridge when I told her *all about Eve*. Joan said it was all lies. HA! We argued. We cussed. We said nasty no-no words. Then she grabbed the wheel.

(*While* **BETTE** *is acting out her words, behind her* **JOAN** *is imitating the same actions.*)

I grabbed it back. She grabbed it again! The bitch was persistent! The car spun out of control and went over the bridge.

JOAN. When I awoke we were in the hospital. Bette had received only a few minor scratches and the *face* you see now.

(*melodramatically, indicating wheelchair*)

I was left the way you see me!

(regaining composure)

Anyway, during those long months of our recuperation, we were visited daily by the Sisters of San Andreas. We decided to join the Order and they taught us a whole new way of life.

*(**HATTIE** enters from bedroom hallway searching under the furniture, carrying a baseball bat.)*

HATTIE. Here, Toto. Here, Toto. Where is that battery-powered pooch?

(to the others)

You ought to see what he's done to my hallway floor. He's left little Ever-Readys everywhere!

*(**HATTIE** crosses behind sofa, still looking for Toto, she kneels down until she is hidden from the audience.)*

*(**JOAN** and **BETTE** start to exit towards bedroom hallway.)*

*(**BETTE** lets out a very loud hiccough.)*

JOAN. Bette, excuse yourself!

*(**BETTE** hiccoughs again.)*

Bette, please!

(another hiccough)

TALLULAH. She must have knocked back that drink too quickly.

JOAN. Sister Hattie, do something.

*(**HATTIE** pops her head up from behind the sofa.)*

HATTIE. Well, what ch'all want me to do about it? I don't know nothin' about *burpin' no Bettes.*

*(**HATTIE** disappears again behind the sofa.)*

JOAN. *(exasperated)* Come along, Bette.

(JOAN and BETTE exit out bedroom hallway. HATTIE rises from behind the sofa, and crosses to the bar. TALLULAH follows JOAN and BETTE out bedroom hallway.)

HATTIE. *(calling after JOAN and BETTE)* You might try putting a bag over her big, powder-puffed head.

(HATTIE puts the baseball bat on the bottom shelf of the bar.)

(TALLULAH stops at bedroom hallway and turns to HATTIE.)

TALLULAH. *(to HATTIE)* Yes dahling, *plastic* should do nicely.

(TALLULAH laughs and exits out bedroom hallway, passing VIVIEN as she enters, fanning herself with her fan.)

VIVIEN. Sister Hattie, I was wondering where you high-tailed it to. I do declare, I think we're going to have a time of it. I don't know about you, but I find some of these Sisters a tad out of the ordinary.

HATTIE. I'll testify to that, Sissy Vivien. I can't believe the way they claw at each other. Maybe you should change tonight's menu from rump roast to Cat Chow.

VIVIEN. You ain't just whistling "Dixie" either. By the way, when is supper being served?

HATTIE. Well that depends, whenever you plan on cooking it.

VIVIEN. You mean you haven't even started it yet? Ooo...

(VIVIEN runs out kitchen hallway.)

HATTIE. That girl catches on real quick.

(Offstage VIVIEN screams and then immediately re-enters running towards HATTIE.)

VIVIEN. Sister Hattie, Sister Hattie!

(**VIVIEN** *jumps into* **HATTIE**'s *arms.*)

Save me! There's a mad woman in there!

(**GLORIA** *enters from kitchen hallway wearing a chef's hat, carrying an oversized meat cleaver in one hand and an hors d'oeuvre tray with sliced salami and cheese on crackers in the other.*)

HATTIE. Lord have mercy!

GLORIA. I can't go on with this meal, Sister DeMille. I'm too happy. Do you mind if I say a few words?

(**HATTIE** *and* **VIVIEN** *shake their heads "no" fearfully.* **GLORIA** *swings the cleaver toward them in a broad gesture as* **HATTIE** *and* **VIVIEN** *duck to avoid it.*)

Thank you.

(**HATTIE** *lowers* **VIVIEN** *to the floor.*)

(to audience)

I just want to tell you all how happy I am to be back in the *pantry* making a *platter* again. You don't know how much I've missed all of you, and I promise, I'll never *dessert* you again. Because after *salami,* we'll make another platter, and another platter. You see, this is my life. It always has been. It always will be. There's nothing else. Just us, the cheese, and those wonderful little crackers out there in the dark.

(**GLORIA** *offers platter to* **HATTIE** *and* **VIVIEN**.)

Hors d'oeuvre?

(**HATTIE** *and* **VIVIEN** *shake their heads "no."*)

GLORIA. *(cont.)* If you need me, I'll be serving the other guests...

(**GLORIA** *swings the cleaver over their heads. They duck again.*)

...on the balcony.

(GLORIA dramatically ascends stairs and offers crackers to various inanimate objects on the balcony.)

VIVIEN. I swear, she's got splinters in the windmills of her mind.

(HATTIE exits out kitchen hallway as MAE and KATHARINE enter from bedroom hallway.)

KATHARINE. *(calling out to VIVIEN)* Oh, Sister Vivien, I was just telling Sister Mae that this place reminds me of my family home in Philadelphia. Have I ever told you about the time I lived in Philadelphia?

(MAE sits pulling KATHARINE down on the sofa with her.)

MAE. Not now, Sister.

VIVIEN. *(making conversation)* So tell me Sisters, what do you all do for the Order?

KATHARINE. I'm the speech therapist.

VIVIEN. Of course. And you, Sister?

MAE. Sex therapist. How 'bout you, honey?

VIVIEN. Sister Hattie and I are in charge of Sister O'Hara's Home for Wayward Rebels.

(GLORIA descends stairs behind the group and eavesdrops as VIVIEN, KATHARINE and MAE gossip.)

MAE. *(thinking aloud)* O'Hara? O'Hara?

(pause)

Isn't that the Sister that fell by the wayside and became a woman of ill repute?

KATHARINE. That reminds me of a friend I had in Philadelphia...

MAE. *(to KATHARINE)* Not now, Sister.

(to VIVIEN)

Continue Sister Vivien.

VIVIEN. Well...she became a destitute prostitute. She ended up marrying one of her johns...Wayne. The last I heard, they ran off to Iwo Jima and had a son who turned out to be... *(looking side-to-side scandalously)* homosexual.

MAE. They raised a *fag* on Iwo Jima?

(VIVIEN nods "yes." GLORIA leans in and offers the tray to KATHARINE, VIVIEN and MAE.)

GLORIA. Hors d'oeuvre?

VIVIEN. *(leery)* Heavens no.

KATHARINE. *(also skeptical)* I just couldn't.

(GLORIA loudly brings the cleaver down on the platter. They each take a cracker quickly.)

VIVIEN, KATHARINE & MAE. *(afraid)* Well, maybe just one.

MAE. Sister Gloria, I think I hear a box of Triscuits calling your name.

(VIVIEN hides her mouth with her fan.)

VIVIEN. Gloria! Gloria!

(Mistaking VIVIEN's voice as a voice calling her from off stage, GLORIA glances towards the kitchen hallway. They all throw their crackers back on the platter.)

MAE. Why don't you go out to the kitchen and come back later?

GLORIA. Comeback! I hate that word. It's return! A return to the millions of people who've never forgiven me for deserting the pantry.

(GLORIA vamps towards the kitchen hallway. She stops and looks back.)

GLORIA. *(cont.)* I will return.

MAE. Lucky us.

(GLORIA *exits to kitchen hallway.* JOAN *enters from bedroom hallway with the birdcage in her lap. She crosses to center stage.*)

JOAN. Hello Sisters. Have any of you seen my sister, Bette? She was supposed to feed Pookie and clean his cage.

KATHARINE. I believe I saw her in the library.

JOAN. I'll ring for her.

(*They all look toward the bedroom hallway.* JOAN *repeatedly presses an actual working buzzer on the arm of the wheelchair. The others slowly look quizzically from the bedroom hallway to* JOAN. JOAN *stops pressing the buzzer.*)

So...is everyone settled in?

KATHARINE. I find it quite comfortable, don't you? So peaceful. It reminds me of my home in Philadelphia. Have I ever told you about the time I lived in Phila...

(MAE *throws the end of her boa into* KATHARINE*'s face.* KATHARINE *pulls the feathers off the tip of her tongue.*)

JOAN. (*interrupting* KATHARINE) I wonder what can be keeping my sister.

(JOAN *presses the buzzer repeatedly.*)

(BETTE *enters from bedroom hallway wearing curlers, a bathrobe and slippers, holding a lit cigarette and a copy of Daily Variety.*)

BETTE. (*agitated*) Stop with that frigging buzzer!

(JOAN *stops pressing the buzzer.*)

What d'ya want?

JOAN. Bette, Pookie and I are hungry.

BETTE. Well, of course you're hungry. You didn't eatcha' dinner last night. That's why you're hungry.

JOAN. But we didn't stop for breakfast this morning.

BETTE. Of course we didn't stop for breakfast. Because you didn't eat your din-din.

JOAN. You're trying to starve us.

(**BETTE** *crosses to* **JOAN.**)

BETTE. Oh, I'm sorry, sister. Is little Pookie angry with me?

(**BETTE** *leans toward birdcage and flicks her cigarette over bird.*)

(*malevolently*) Here kitty, kitty, KITTY!

(**BETTE** *laughs maniacally and exits to bedroom hallway.*)

JOAN. (*to* **POOKIE**) There, there, Pookie. Auntie Bette didn't mean it.

(*embarrassed*) I'd like to apologize again for my sister, Sisters. I don't know what's gotten into her lately. She's so tense and irritable.

KATHARINE. It's probably the pressures of living in a big city. I lived in a big city once. Philadelphia. Have I ever told you...

JOAN. (*exasperated*) Not again, Sister Katharine...

(*All offstage Sisters lean in various doorways and join with* **JOAN,** **VIVIEN** *and* **MAE**...)

ALL. ...not the *Philadelphia story!*

(*The Sisters then re-exit offstage.* **HATTIE** *enters from kitchen hallway pulling a long rope which is attached to a flat furniture dolly, rolling on four casters. On top of the dolly is* **GLORIA** *who is reclining while "eating" a fake loaf of bread. She conceals a white dusting cloth.*)

HATTIE. If you all don't keep this psycho out of my kitchen, I'm gonna fricassee her niblets.

(**HATTIE** *shoves* **GLORIA** *off the dolly and carries it back to the kitchen.*)

VIVIEN. Now calm yourself down, Sister Hattie. Excuse me, Sisters.

(**VIVIEN** *follows* **HATTIE** *out kitchen hallway.*)

(**GLORIA** *begins to clean the floor with a white dusting cloth.*)

GLORIA. WAX!...MAX!...WAX! Dirty, yellow wax buildup. I won't tolerate it. What would Valentino say?

(**JUDY** *enters from bedroom hallway with a barking* **Toto** *on a leash. She pulls and/or kicks him along.*)

(**JUDY** *acknowledges each Sister then stops next to* **GLORIA** *with* **Toto** *barking continuously near* **GLORIA**'s *face.*)

JUDY. Sister...Sister...Sister...Sister. Toto and I are going out for a walk down that yellow brick path. Would anyone care to join us?

GLORIA. My God...we've got barking little people!

(**GLORIA** *whacks* **Toto** *with the loaf of bread.*)

(**JUDY** *picks* **Toto** *up and clutches him to her.*)

JUDY. Why, you wicked old witch. Why don't you pick on someone your own size?

(**JUDY** *tries to slap* **GLORIA**'s *nose.*)

GLORIA. Very well...

(**GLORIA** *starts to hit* **JUDY** *with the loaf of bread.*)

(*Frightened,* **JUDY** *turns and runs up stairs.*)

JUDY. (*shouting*) Auntie Em! Uncle Henry! Auntie Em!

(*As* **JUDY** *reaches the balcony, the offstage front door bursts open. Leaves and debris are blown into the hallway as the sound of a* **tornado** *is heard.* **JUDY** *fights against it. The other Sisters sway with the wind.*)

(shouting to be heard above tornado)

It's a twister, Sisters! It's a twister, Sisters!

*(**JUDY** exits. The front door closes and the **tornado** cuts out.)*

(The other Sisters regain composure.)

MAE. Poor little kid. I hope she gets home all right.

*(**JOAN** points to the floor near **GLORIA**.)*

JOAN. *(obsessive)* Look, Sisters. She missed a spot. Gloria, you missed a spot. Now, I'm not mad at you. I'm mad at the dirt.

*(**JOAN** pulls a toothbrush and a can of cleanser from her purse and hands them to **GLORIA**.)*

Here, a toothbrush and a little Bon Ami will do wonders.

*(**GLORIA** quickly "sprinkles" a little cleanser on the floor then hands the toothbrush and cleanser back to **JOAN**. Using the white dusting cloth, **GLORIA** "cleans" madly moving towards **KATHARINE** and **MAE** on the sofa. **GLORIA** growls like a polishing machine. **KATHARINE** and **MAE** rise and move away from her.)*

MAE. *(indicating **GLORIA**)* I think she's spending too much time downwind of that powdered cleanser.

*(Trying to "clear the room" and get away from **GLORIA**)*

Why don't we go see if Sister Vivien needs any help setting up for the ceremony?

*(**KATHARINE** and **MAE** rise and skirt around **GLORIA**.)*

KATHARINE AND JOAN. That's a good idea, Sister Mae.

KATHARINE. That's the Holywood spirit, sisters. Everyone utilizing their energies to succeed in one great endeavor. Just like my ancestors who came to these shores on the Mayflower.

(**KATHARINE** *exits to the kitchen hallway.*)

MAE. *(to* **JOAN***)* Pity it wasn't the Titanic.

(**MAE** *pushes* **JOAN***'s wheelchair as they exit to the kitchen hallway. Immediately,* **TALLULAH** *enters from the bedroom hallway and crosses to the bar.*)

TALLULAH. *(to* **GLORIA***, with a sweeping motion)* One side, dahling, this girl needs a drink. By the way, you're doing a marvelous job.

GLORIA. Valentino's coming.

TALLULAH. I'll alert the media.

(*Using the dustcloth as a marker,* **GLORIA** *begins to play hopscotch on the balcony tile as* **TALLULAH** *begins to make a drink.* **MARILYN** *enters from the bedroom hallway.*)

MARILYN. *(waving her hand)* Yoo-hoo, Sister Tallulah!

TALLULAH. Ah, Sister Marilyn, gyrate those hips to the bar and have a toddy for the body.

(**MARILYN** *crosses to bar eying* **GLORIA** *cautiously and sits on the stage right barstool.*)

MARILYN. That sounds marvelous, but…

(*indicating* **GLORIA**)

…whatever *she's* drinking, I don't want any.

(**GLORIA** *continues to play hopscotch out the front entranceway as* **JUDY** *re-enters carrying* **Toto***, her basket and a large pill bottle.* **The Munchkin's Tune** *is heard. A spotlight hits her, accentuating her new attire. She is now wearing red ruby slippers with blue bobby socks and a blue and white-checkered dress in the same style as the previous black and white-checkered one. Her lipstick is a bright red and she is now wearing rouge.* **JUDY** *stands at the top of the stairs admiring her "new" dress and slippers.*)

TALLULAH. That must be the horse of a different color I've heard tell about.

(**JUDY** *pops a pill into her mouth.* **The Munchkin's Tune** *fades out.*)

(*with a sweeping motion*) Sister Judy, dahling, come on down here. Forget your troubles. Come on. Get happy.

(**JUDY** *descends the stairs quickly, crosses to the bar and sits on the stage left bar stool.*)

(**TALLULAH** *pours her a drink.*)

Here. This should put you over the rainbow. So tell me, Sisters, how do you like our quaint surroundings?

JUDY. Oh, I just love it. And so does Toto. We've never been to a place like this before.

TOTO. Bark, bark, bark, bark.

JUDY. *(to TOTO)* Oh, that's right Toto...except for that bad acid trip to the Emerald City.

TALLULAH. *(dryly)* Yes...And what *planet* are you from Sister Marilyn?

MARILYN. I'm just a girl from Nantucket,
who got fed up with life and said fu...

(**JUDY** *is shocked.*)

JUDY. *(interrupting)* Oh, my!

MARILYN. Then someone broke my heart in D.C.;
cuz he wouldn't leave his wife for me.
Like a little lost lamb, I roamed about;
then I joined the Order and became devout.

TALLULAH. My Gawd! How can someone's life have rhyme but no reason?

JUDY. *(to MARILYN)* What made you join the Order, Sister?

(**MARILYN** *rises as the lights dim. A spotlight illuminates her as she moves center stage.*)

(**TALLULAH** *reacts in surprise as the stage lights dim.*)

MARILYN. *(to audience, with foreboding)* Well, late one night, I found myself in a sleazy, rundown motel called the *Misfit Inn*. It was near a *bus stop* at the foot of the *Montgomery Cliffs*. And as I penetrated the building...

JUDY. *(interrupting)* Oh, no, Sister Marilyn, that's *entered...entered* the building.

MARILYN. *(to* **JUDY***)* Oh, gee thanks ever so.

(to audience)

As I *entered* the building, a group of vile, drunken men approached me, wearing Detroit Tiger and Lion team-jackets. They teased me and said the filthiest things.

(shuddering)

It was icky.

(to audience)

Well it was.

(back to story)

The next thing I knew, they threw me to the floor and ripped off all my clothes!

JUDY. Lions and tigers...

MARILYN. *(covering herself)* ...and bare!

TALLULAH & JUDY. *(in unison)* Oh, my!

JUDY. What did you do then?

MARILYN. Fortunately, nearby was Sister Jackie Chan.

*(**MARILYN** performs some karate gestures.)*

He heard my screams, came to my rescue, and beat the crap out of them. It inspired me to join the Order and it became my first real home.

*(Lighting returns to normal as **MARILYN** returns to her barstool.)*

TALLULAH. Your fifteen minutes of fame are up, dahling.

(to **JUDY***)*

All right, it's your turn.

JUDY. *(excitedly)* And Toto, too?

TALLULAH. *(dryly)* Whatever.

JUDY. Well, as a teenager, I was a member of a sister
Sister act. We weren't very good.

TALLULAH. *(knowingly to the audience)* I know.

JUDY. Then I went solo and became rich beyond my
wildest dreams.

(growing serious)

But I found out that money doesn't buy happiness.

MARILYN. *(dumbfounded)* It doesn't?

JUDY. No. It can also buy self-destruction.

(distraught)

Toto and I developed an addiction to...cocaine!

MARILYN. *(shocked)* Toto toots, too?

JUDY. Toto tooted, too.

*(***JUDY** *rises as the lights start to dim, placing Toto
on top of the bar.* **TALLULAH** *reacts ala "here we go
again" as the lights dim.)*

(A spotlight illuminates **JUDY** *as she completes her
cross to center stage.)*

One night, while we were on tour, Toto and I got
totally coked up at a party. I had no business getting behind the wheel of a car, but...

(accusing and pointing at **TOTO***)*

JUDY. *(cont.)* ...Toto, yah, it was Toto...Toto insisted
that I drive.

TALLULAH. *(Hits* **TOTO** *on the head with the baseball bat.)*
Bad, Toto, Bad!

*(***JUDY** *hears the commotion, turns to look towards
bar.)*

(**TALLULAH** *has quickly replaced the baseball bat behind the bar and gives an innocent look to* **JUDY**.)

JUDY. *(back to audience)* The next thing I knew, I lost control of the car and ran over a family of munchkins.

MARILYN. Oh, you poor kid.

JUDY. Well, I didn't know I'd hit them...I thought they were speed bumps. We knew we had to change our ways or we'd end up in the gutter...just like you Sister Tallulah.

(**TALLULAH** *slams her drink down on the bar and glares at* **JUDY**.)

(quickly) So, we joined the Order and we've been with them ever since.

(The lighting restores as **JUDY** *curtsies and returns to her barstool.* **VIVIEN** *enters from kitchen hallway.)*

VIVIEN. *(agitated)* Well, where is everyone? It's almost time for our rehearsal.

(**GLORIA** *enters through the front entranceway carrying a lawn flamingo that wears a sheik's headdress.* **GLORIA** *conceals a red rose.)*

GLORIA. Valentino, I'm so glad you could make it to our party. I love what you're wearing. It makes you look so *(pause) sheik*. And weren't you taller the last time we danced the Tango?

(We hear **Tango** *music as* **GLORIA** *and* **VALENTINO** *dance down the stairs and around the room.)*

MARILYN. She's adjusted so well here. She's already found a new little friend.

TALLULAH. And they're both tuned in to the same channel.

(**GLORIA** *puts the red rose between her teeth and grabs* **VIVIEN**. *The* **Tango** *music continues as*

GLORIA *performs an exaggerated tango dance around the room with the startled and dumbstruck* VIVEN *and "Valentino."* TALLULAH *and* MARILYN *are oblivious to the music and the dance.)*

*(*TALLULAH *places a bottle of alcohol on the shelf behind the bar. She notices the framed poem entitled "Ten Sisters of San Andreas" which is also located on a shelf behind the bar. She takes it down and begins to read to herself.* MARILYN *notices the china nun ring and crosses to them.* JUDY *pops a pill and watches* GLORIA *and* VIVIEN *tango.* JUDY *is enjoying the spectacle. At the conclusion of the dance,* GLORIA *and* VIVIEN *tango out the kitchen hallway as the* **Tango** *music ends.)*

VIVIEN. *(over her shoulder as she and* GLORIA *exit)* This place is an insane asylum!

MARILYN. *(referring to the china nun ring)* Aren't they sweet?

*(*MARILYN *points to the ring of ten, six-inch-high china nuns sitting on the pedestal.)*

Those little china nuns.

TALLULAH. Sisters, listen to this.

(reading aloud)

'Ten Sisters of San Andreas playing with a vine,
One went and hung herself, and then there were nine.'

*(*MARILYN *takes her reading glasses out of her purse and puts them on. She crosses to* TALLULAH *and takes the poem from her.)*

MARILYN. *(reading aloud)* 'Nine Sisters of San Andreas all playing with fate,
One went for bust, and then there were eight.'

JUDY. Let Toto read one.

(**MARILYN** *holds the poem for Toto to "read." He barks repeatedly until* **TALLULAH** *grabs the poem away indignantly.*)

TALLULAH. *(interrupting)* Give me that!

(reading aloud)

'Eight Sisters of San Andreas aiming for heaven, One became a centerfold, and then there were seven.'

(**VIVIEN** *enters from kitchen hallway in a huff, followed by* **HATTIE.**)

VIVIEN. *(angrily)* Are any of you broads gonna participate in our rehearsal for the opening ceremony?

(**HATTIE** *indicates to her watch.*)

TALLULAH. *(to* **VIVIEN***)* Your excursion through menopause is turning out to be a tad turbulent, isn't it dahling?

(**JUDY** *offers pill bottle to* **VIVIEN.** **VIVIEN** *pulls out a gun from behind her back.* **TALLULAH, MARILYN** *and* **JUDY** *gasp and stare at the gun.*)

VIVIEN. My "Yankee Killer" and I insist you join us in the kitchen – NOW!

(**VIVIEN** *shoots the gun in the air.* **TALLULAH, MARILYN** *and* **JUDY** *rush toward the kitchen hallway knocking into* **VIVIEN** *and* **HATTIE.** *They ad-lib "Get out of my way, she's crazy...")*

(composing herself, while speaking to **HATTIE***)*

Well, I know what they're saying about me, and frankly my dear, I don't give a damn.

HATTIE. *(mumbling)* It ain't fittin'. It just ain't fittin.'

(**VIVIEN** *hands the gun to* **HATTIE.** **HATTIE** *raises her skirt and bright red petticoat to reveal a leg holster and places the gun in the holster.* **HATTIE** *then* *exits thru kitchen doorway.* **VIVIEN** *crosses to the Victrola, cranks the handle and lowers the needle to play a record.)*

VIVIEN. Oh, Mother Paramount is just going to love this. This number is sure to put me up there with the likes of Cardinal Busby Berkeley! *(calling offstage)* OK, Sisters are you ready out there?

*(**VIVIEN** ascends to top of stairs.)*

KATHARINE. *(offstage)* This reminds me of the parades we used to have in...

ALL *(offstage)* **& VIVIEN.** Aw, shut up!

*(**VIVIEN** switches off the lights. Blackout. **Let's Say, "Hooray For Holywood"** music starts. During the music, in the darkness, the Sisters take their places for an all-out Busby Berkeley-style production number, complete with large white feather fans and special lighting.)*

Song – LET'S SAY, 'HOORAY FOR HOLYWOOD'

LET'S SAY "HOORAY
FOR HOLYWOOD!"
WHERE A CAMERA TURNS YOUR GRAMMA
INTO DORIS DAY.
COME, JOIN OUR ORDER
AND YOU CAN BE A STAR IN JUST ONE DAY...
IN HOLYWOOD.
HOORAY!

OPENING NIGHT IS A FABULOUS SIGHT
ESPECIALLY IF YOU'RE "IN THE KNOW."
BUT, BETTER BEWARE
OF THAT GIRL WITH RED HAIR...
SHE'D KILL TO BE IN THE NEXT SHOW.

ALL. *(cont.)*

> LET'S SAY "HOORAY
> FOR HOLYWOOD!"
> WHERE EV'RY LETTER THAT YOU GET INCLUDES
> A RESUME
> COME, JOIN OUR ORDER
> AND YOU CAN BE A STAR IN JUST ONE DAY...
> IN HOLYWOOD.
> HOORAY!

> *(instrumental break)*

> HITCHCOCK AND ZANUCK
> CAN BE QUITE GERMANIC
> WHENEVER THEY'RE PITCHING A SHOW.
> BUT THEY'RE ALWAYS NICE
> WHEN THEY HEAR THE RIGHT PRICE
> AND THEIR BACKERS ALL TELL THEM "LET'S GO!"

> LET'S SAY "HOORAY...
> HOORAY! HOORAY
> FOR HOLYWOOD!"
> WHERE IT'S TRENDY TO BE FRIENDLY
> 'TIL YOU GET YOUR WAY.

> COME, JOIN OUR ORDER
> AND YOU CAN BE A STAR IN JUST ONE DAY...
> IN HOLYWOOD.
> HOORAY!

*(At the completion of the dance, **JOAN** holds up a cutout of the Paramount mountain, in honor of Mother Paramount. The Sisters finish by forming a half circle around **JOAN** and hold the feather fans outwards to resemble the stars that border the Paramount mountain. When the production number finishes, the Sisters congratulate themselves as **MAE** and **BETTE** gather all the feather fans and clear them off stage. They immediately re-enter. Suddenly, the lights start to flicker and a mysterious **witch's voice** is heard.)*

THE WITCH'S VOICE. *(V.O.)* *(loud cackle)* Quiet my little pretties. Sisters of San Andreas, it is time to face your judge and jury.

(Everyone looks and/or points to the Victrola in shock as they realize **THE WITCH'S VOICE** *is coming from the record! As* **THE WITCH'S VOICE** *continues, each Sister reacts as her name is mentioned. The other Sisters look at each Sister as they are named.)*

THE WITCH'S VOICE. *(V.O.)* You have been charged with these indictments. That you did respectively and at diverse times break one of the sacred Ten Directions of the moral code of the Order. Sister Vivien, that you did joyfully step on peons on your climb to near the top of the Order; Sister Mae, that you did vulcanize your volcanoes; Sister Tallulah, that you did party with Bacardi in the bed of Andy Hardy; Sister Judy, that you did turn little people into hood ornaments. Sister Gloria, that you did dwell in the house of narcotics...

*(***GLORIA** *raises her closed fist to her mouth and coughs some white powder into the air.)*

...Sister Katharine, that you did shoot loons out of season; Sister Marilyn, that you did unfold your folds in a foldout; Sister Joan, that you did force your fellow Sisters to buy Amway products; Sister Hattie, that you actually own an entire collection of Wayne Newton albums...

(They all gasp loudly.)

...Sister Bette, that you are such a bitch...

(The record begins to skip, repeating the last two words, over and over.)

"a bitch...a bitch...a bitch..."

*(***MAE** *rushes to the Victrola and bumps it with her hip to "fix" the skip.)*

(The dialogue continues.)

Prisoners at the bar, you have been found guilty as charged and you shall all pay for your transgressions. *(pause)* But that's not what's worrying me; it's how to do it. These things must be done delicately. Drat you all, you've been more trouble to me than you're worth. Remember, the last to go will see the first nine go before her...and that mangy little dog, too. So don't leave my pretties, why, my little dinner party is just beginning.

(THE WITCH'S VOICE *lets out a high-pitched, cackling laugh. It continues until the record is turned off.)*

(JUDY *screams and faints face down on the floor.* **Toto** *is on the floor, barking.)*

(TALLULAH *pours herself another drink.)*

(MAE *takes the record off the turntable.)*

(MARILYN *fans* **JUDY** *with her (* **MARILYN***'s) dress.)*

JOAN. Is this some kind of prank? Who put that record on? Who was that speaking?

BETTE. It's obviously a disgraceful and harmful practical joke.

(pause)

I couldn't have done it better myself.

MAE. You think it's a joke, do you?

(MARILYN *bends down to help* **JUDY** *stand up.)*

MARILYN. What else could it be?

JUDY. Did I faint, Sister Marilyn?

MARILYN. Either that or you were frenching the floor.

VIVIEN. That's not the record I put on.

(MARILYN *helps* **JUDY** *to the sofa.)*

(JOAN *grabs the record from* **MAE.***)*

JOAN. What does it say on the label?

(**KATHARINE** *grabs the record from* **JOAN**.)

KATHARINE. 'Th-th-th-th-th-th-that's All Folks.'

(**JUDY** *grabs the record from* **KATHARINE**. **VIVIEN** *grabs the record from* **JUDY**. **HATTIE** *grabs it from* **VIVIEN** *who immediately grabs it back. It passes back down the line ending with* **JOAN**. *Meanwhile, the dialogue continues.*)

BETTE. It seems to me that someone's trying to scare the wits out of us. And I demand to know why!

(**GLORIA** *grabs the record from* **JOAN**.)

JOAN. What if we're not alone on the island? Perhaps there's a madman hiding out there!

MAE. That wouldn't be so bad, would it?

(**GLORIA** *puts the record on the tip of a pen and spins it like a circus juggling act.*)

GLORIA. Round and round and round she goes...who gets killed...no one knows!

BETTE. Give me that! Here, Lassie, fetch!

(**BETTE** *grabs the record from* **GLORIA** *and throws it, likes a Frisbee, out the front entranceway.*)

(**GLORIA** *runs out after it.*)

KATHARINE. You know, Sister Joan had a point there. We must organize ourselves just like our forefathers did in Philadelphia. Did I ever tell you about the time..?

TALLULAH. You do and you'll be the first to go!

JOAN. Stop it you two. Stop bickering. Now let's all just calm down and think about this.

(**GLORIA** *re-enters from the front entranceway with the record in her mouth.*)

Sit down. Sit down, everyone.

(**GLORIA** *runs and sits next to* **JOAN**, *still with the record in her mouth.*)

(**BETTE** *sits on the sofa and the other Sisters sit around the room.*)

JOAN. *(cont.)* *(to* **GLORIA***)* Stay! Good girl.

(**JOAN** *pats* **GLORIA** *on the head as* **GLORIA** *scratches behind her ear.* **BETTE** *takes a box of chocolates from table behind sofa and begins to eat them as* **JOAN** *looks on hungrily.* **GLORIA** *rises and crosses to sit next to* **VIVIEN** *on the stairs and mimics her using the record as a fan; then as a steering wheel on a racing car. After a few seconds,* **JUDY** *closes her eyes and begins to click her heels together three times. She opens her eyes and realizes that she is still in the room. She closes her eyes and repeats the three clicks. She opens her eyes again.*)

JUDY. *(frustrated)* Shit!!

(**JUDY** *continues to click her heels in groups of three, each time building in intensity. As the clicking continues,* **BETTE** *becomes more agitated.* **MARILYN** *moves to the rhythm of the clicking shoes.*)

BETTE. *(irritated)* Will you stop it!

(**BETTE** *jumps up while throwing the box of candy in* **JOAN***'s lap, who begins to devour it ravenously.*)

(to **JUDY***)*

I can't take it any longer! Must you keep click, click, clicking your heels!?

JUDY. Do you mind!? I'm trying to get home here.

(yelling at her shoes)

Magic slippers, my ass!

BETTE. *(pointing her extended fingers ala the Wicked Witch of the West)* Give me those ruby slippers!

JUDY. *(to* **BETTE***)* But I wanna go home.

(to **MARILYN***)*

I wanna go home.

MARILYN. *(waves at* **JUDY***)* Bye.

JUDY. *(Back to* **BETTE***. Getting hysterical.)* I wanna go home.

*(***BETTE*** slaps* **JUDY** *across the face.)*

BETTE. Aw, shut up!

*(***JUDY*** jumps up and faces* **BETTE***.)*

JUDY. Why you wicked old witch! I'll…I'll drop a house on you!

*(***BETTE*** pushes her back.)*

BETTE. Oh, yeah! You and what tornado!?

*(***BETTE*** turns away and* **JUDY** *pushes her. All the Sisters react and gasp.)*

*(***BETTE*** slowly turns toward* **JUDY** *ala the "Niagara Falls" bit…slowly I turn, step by step…)*

You…rotten…little…Gumm…sister!

(All the Sisters gasp a bit louder.)

JUDY. *Jezebel!*

(All the Sisters gasp loudly. **GLORIA** *raps her fist on the bar and begins to chant.)*

GLORIA. Fight. Fight. Fight.

*(***BETTE*** and* **JUDY** *begin to fight.* **MAE** *and* **KATHA- RINE** *separate them as* **VIVIEN** *crosses center stage.)*

VIVIEN. *(hysterical)* Hush up! Now, if there is anyone on this island we'll find him. He can't go very far. I'm not going to let anyone spoil my chances of impressing Mother Paramount.

(Suddenly worried, **VIVIEN** *looks into the mirror.)*

(composing herself)

Heavens, if there is a perverted intruder on this island, I can't let him see me like this. I need to put on more makeup.

(**TALLULAH** *holds up a garden trowel from behind the bar.*)

TALLULAH. *(to **VIVIEN**)* Would you like to borrow my trowel?

(**VIVIEN** *glares at* **TALLULAH**)

KATHARINE. Sister Mae, you stay here with Sister Judy. She's still very pale...

*(to **BETTE**)*

...except for a little red handprint.

(**MAE** *crosses to* **JUDY. JUDY** *leans on* **MAE**'s *shoulder.*)

MAE. Of course. I'll take good care of her.

KATHARINE. Good. Sisters...let's move out!

(All the Sisters begin to exit.)

(**BETTE** *sees* **JOAN** *frantically shoving the candy in her mouth, and snatches it away from her.*)

BETTE. Give me that!

(**BETTE** *ascends balcony to entranceway.* **JOAN** *tries to follow her, but can only spin her wheelchair around at the bottom of the stairs in a pathetic little circle.*)

JOAN. *(pleading)* Oh, Bette. Bette, please. Please leave the candy. Oh, Bette, please. I'm starving. Please.

(**BETTE** *pauses at the entranceway, looks at* **JOAN**, *taunts her with a piece of candy, then pops it into her own mouth.*)

BETTE. Sorry.

(**BETTE** *exits out front entranceway.* **JOAN** *wheels out bedroom hallway, sobbing.*)

(**JUDY** *gets pill bottle from basket. She is so nervous, that she shakes the bottle while trying to open it. The pills rattle loudly.*)

(**MAE** *reaches her hands out to stop the shaking; takes the pill bottle, opens it, takes out a couple of pills and hands them to* **JUDY**.)

MAE. *(comforting* **JUDY**) Oh, are you all right honey? It looks like you just saw a ghost...of Orson Welles... naked.

(**JUDY** *swallows the pills that* **MAE** *gave to her and puts the bottle back in her basket.*)

JUDY. Oh, I'm okay, but I must look a fright. And Toto, too.

(frightened) Sister Mae, why is that wicked old witch doing this to us?

MAE. Obviously, dearie, in her eyes we're all sinners and she's about to dole out justice.

JUDY. Are you guilty, too?

MAE. *(indicating her chest)* The mistakes of my frivolous youth.

JUDY. You mean...?

MAE. I guess you could say I falsified my credentials. I had 'em done when I was eighteen. That year June wasn't the only thing busting out all over...so was Mae. Now don't worry about it honey, everything will be just fine. You follow your instructions and I promise no harm will come to you. Now calm down, pop a couple of valiums, and try to find a place where there isn't any trouble.

(**JUDY** *heads for the stairs. She drops Toto on the floor, while still holding onto his leash, and reaches in her basket for her pill bottle.*)

JUDY. A place where there isn't any trouble?

(**JUDY** *crosses up stairs to front entranceway. While still holding onto his leash, Toto "bumps" up each stair. She opens bottle and pops a pill into her mouth.*)

JUDY. *(cont.)* Do you think there is such a place, Toto? There must be. It isn't a place you can get to by a boat, or a train, or even a trolley. And I've tried, dammit, I've tried!

*(**MAE** turns away from **JUDY** and ignores her.)*

It's far, far away...beyond the moon...beyond the rain...

*(Suddenly, a black-gloved hand reaches in from behind the front entranceway, covers **JUDY**'s mouth, and pulls her offstage. **MAE** is oblivious.)*

*(Immediately the **Mystery Track (spooky)** plays as the lights dim. **MAE** looks around the room, making sure that she is alone and crosses to the coffee service. She extracts a vial from her bosom, and pours a liquid into the coffee pot. **MAE** exits out kitchen hallway.)*

*(**BETTE** enters from the bedroom hallway and crosses up to the closet. From behind her back, **BETTE** produces a small gold statue that matches an existing one located on a pedestal near the closet and exchanges them. **BETTE** exits through the front entranceway.)*

*(**KATHARINE** enters quickly from the kitchen hallway wearing a lampshade with fringe on her head and stands against the wall for a moment as though she were disguising herself as a floor lamp. The fringe sways with her head-shaking movements. She performs a variety of thrust and parry moves with two 12" tent spikes. She crosses to stage left, occasionally bumping into furniture and runs into the wall. **KATHARINE** exits, finally, out bedroom hallway.)*

*(The closet curtain opens and **GLORIA** sticks her head out.)*

GLORIA. Peek-a-boo!

(**GLORIA** *looks around and then retreats back into the closet, closing the curtain behind her.*)

(*Simultaneously* **TALLULAH** *and* **JOAN** *try to enter from opposite sides of the room, discover each other and then both back out. They repeat this once more and both back out again.* **JOAN** *finally enters from bedroom hallway alone and wheels to the sofa. She moves a sofa cushion and produces a screwdriver. Using the screwdriver, she fiddles with the buzzer on her wheelchair.* **JOAN** *replaces the screwdriver under the sofa cushion and exits to bedroom hallway.*)

(**TALLULAH** *enters from kitchen hallway with a hangman's noose and grabs a drink off the bar.* **TALLULAH** *laughs and exits up the stairs and out the front entranceway.*)

(**MARILYN** *enters from kitchen hallway carrying a large knife. She tiptoes to the closet, places the knife under her arm, opens the closet curtain, pulls the knife out apparently cutting herself. While covering her mouth to stifle a scream, she quickly hides the knife in the closet, closes the curtain and exits out the front entranceway.*)

(**VIVIEN** *enters from the bedroom hallway and crosses to the telephone. She pulls a large pair of scissors from her bodice and snips the telephone cord. After making sure the line is dead, she replaces the scissors back into her bodice, cutting herself. She grimaces and rushes out the kitchen hallway.*)

(*The 8' tall gold statue opens and* **HATTIE** *enters from the secret passageway. She pulls up her skirt and bright red petticoat, revealing a gun in a holster strapped to her leg. She removes the gun, and stands poised, ready to shoot. "Covering the room,"* **HATTIE** *backs out and exits through kitchen hallway.*)

*(The lights fade to Blackout. In the darkness, **The Witch's Cackle** is heard. The lights come up and the **Mystery Track (spooky)** fades out. Immediately All, but **JUDY**, enter from where they last exited.)*

JOAN. Did you hear that?

*(The Sisters loudly ad-lib the results of their "search" for the killer. **JOAN** presses her buzzer repeatedly.)*

BETTE. Will everybody shut up!

*(to **JOAN**, irritated)*

And stop with that frigging buzzer!

*(**JOAN** stops pressing the buzzer.)*

HATTIE. We scoured this entire Catalina-wanna-be from top to bottom and the only things on this island are nine waddlin' penguin-fools and a black goddess.

VIVIEN. This whole thing just doesn't make any sense.

KATHARINE. But it does. It's all very elementary. Obviously one of us perpetrated this prank.

(All adlib shock and disagreement.)

MARILYN. Stop it! Stop it! I can't take anymore. I don't like this kind of game.

*(**MARILYN** crosses to phone and picks up the receiver.)*

I'm going to call for someone to take me off this icky island. *(into phone)* Hello, John. Hello, Bobby, Hello Jackie...Ohhh!

*(**MARILYN** notices the phone line has been cut and holds up the severed cord.)*

(shocked) Someone's circumcised the cord!

TALLULAH. My Gawd, an enemy among us?! I need a drink.

GLORIA. Infidels behind our lines? Why didn't anybody tell me?

(**GLORIA** *reaches into the closet, grabs a WWI army helmet, puts it on her head and pulls out a broom which she holds like a rifle.*)

I'll stand guard.

JOAN. Maybe she needs some fresh air. Sister Marilyn, would you mind opening the window for her please?

MARILYN. Sure, Sister, I'll get it.

KATHARINE. Open a new window. Open a new door.

(**MARILYN** *ascends to balcony to open the drapes.*)

(**TALLULAH** *pulls the cork out of a decanter.*)

TALLULAH. Open a new bottle, dahling.

(*As the drapes open, we hear the sound of a **thunderclap and rumble** and see a flash of **lightning** on* **JUDY** *and **Toto,** each hanging from a hangman's noose on the tree outside of the window.*)

(*All look towards the window in shock and scream.* **MARILYN** *does not realize why everyone is screaming. She puts on her eyeglasses, turns and sees* **JUDY** *and **Toto** hanging.*)

MARILYN. *(shocked)* Screamy-poo!

(**MARILYN** *swoons and falls to the floor.*)

(**GLORIA** *looks out the window and turns to the others.*)

GLORIA. My God! Are we decorating for Christmas? Someone's hung *Garland* on the tree.

(*All Sisters turn in shock to audience, gasp and freeze.*)

(*Blackout*)

End of Act I

ACT II

Scene One

(It is the following morning. The room is the same as the previous night except that the drapes are closed once again.)

*(The house lights go to half. **The Hand Sting with The Witch's Cackle** plays after the house lights go out. A spot light comes up on the Mother Paramount portrait. A black-gloved hand opens the portrait and tips over a nun figurine. The action should be timed so that **The Witch's Cackle** is heard as the portrait is closed. The spot light fades out as the stage lights come up.)*

*(**MAE** enters from the bedroom hallway. She has on a long, sheer robe with balloons as breasts. She conceals a pushpin between her fingers. She carries and is reading a book entitled, "Mae West On Sex." As she enters the room, she stops and turns the book and holds it like a centerfold – scrutinizing "positions" pictured in the book. After she turns the book back to its correct position, she pauses and looks towards the picture window, where we last saw **JUDY** hanging in the tree, and shakes her head.)*

MAE. Poor little Chickadee. What a shame.

*(**MAE** moves toward the bar but stops suddenly. She notices the ring of china nuns and crosses to it. **MAE** picks up the fallen figurine and examines it.)*

What's this? A fallen woman. Oh, honey, do I know that feeling.

(**MAE** *takes a step towards kitchen hallway, sees something, and freezes, registering shock.*)

(*Suddenly, a cloaked arm, holding a gun, appears in the kitchen hallway. A shot is fired.*)

(**MAE** *grabs one of her breasts. The pushpin pops one of the balloons. She spins around in a circle.*)

(*Another shot is fired and* **MAE** *'pops' her other breast, spinning her in the opposite direction. She is left flat.* **MAE** *looks down at the floor, then around the room, crosses to the sofa, picks up a throw pillow, crosses back to her "death" spot and places the pillow on the floor.* **MAE** *drops to her knees – which are now cushioned by the pillow – and looks at her chest.*)

MAE. (*cont.*) Looks like its bedtime for bongos.

(*pause*)

(*and then her famous*)

Oh-h-h-h.

(**MAE** *continues to crumple to the floor.*)

(*We hear the* **The Hand Sting with The Witch's Cackle** *as the lights fade down. A spot light comes up on the Mother Paramount portrait. A black-gloved hand opens the portrait and tips over another nun figurine. Again, the action should be timed so that* **The Witch's Cackle** *is heard as the portrait is closed. The spot light fades out as the stage lights restore.*)

(**HATTIE** *enters from the bedroom hallway, dragging a mop. She looks around to see where the cackle is coming from.*)

HATTIE. What's going on out here? I thought I heard someone shooting off the" Yankee Killer."

(*She sees* **MAE** *on the floor and crosses to her.*)

Oh, so it's you, Sister Mae. Was that you playing with Sister Vivien's "Yankee Killer?" If she finds out she's going to be P.O'd, girlfriend. You know how upset she gets if anyone messes with her piece.

(pause)

HATTIE. *(cont.)* Sister Mae, you ain't said word one since I come in here. I guess you don't function before your first cup of coffee.

(giggles)

Neither do I, child. I'm an evil black woman 'til I've had my half double decaffeinated half-caf, with a twist of lemon.

(HATTIE *bends down and shakes* **MAE.)**

Sister Mae? Sister Mae?

(HATTIE *turns* **MAE** *on her side and screams.)*

(hysterical)

Great day in the morning! She's been deflated! It's murder! Sister Vivien! Sister Vivien! We're all gonna die!

(VIVIEN *enters from bedroom hallway followed by* **MARILYN, JOAN, KATHARINE** *and* **GLORIA. VIVIEN** *crosses to* **HATTIE.)**

VIVIEN. *(to* **HATTIE***)* What's all this commotion?

(TALLULAH *enters the room and surveys the scene.* **HATTIE** *turns* **MAE** *over.)*

HATTIE. It's horrible! Somebody popped her bodacious ta-tas!

VIVIEN. *(gasps)* My God, they are...*gone with the wind.*

(TALLULAH *looks down at* **MAE.)**

TALLULAH. I'm surprised with all that air she didn't fly around the room a couple of times.

(TALLULAH *skips over* **MAE***'s body and crosses to the bar.)*

Anyone for a Bloody Mary?

(VIVIEN *takes the mop from* HATTIE *and exits out the kitchen hallway.*)

KATHARINE. Sister Tallulah, how cold and un-Holywood can you be? Have all your feelings left you?

(TALLULAH *holds up a decanter of liquor.*)

TALLULAH. They will in a minute, dahling.

(GLORIA *crosses to the others.* KATHARINE *leans down to examine the body.*)

KATHARINE. First Sister Judy and now Sister Mae.

(KATHARINE *notices the china nun in* MAE's *hand.*)

What's this?

(KATHARINE *takes the china nun from* MAE's *hand.*)

JOAN. Why, it's one of the china nuns. That silicone bimbo must have broken it.

(GLORIA *sits on the sofa, picks up a book entitled "Swingin' With Swanson" from the sofa table and begins to read.*)

(BETTE, *wearing sunglasses, enters from the front entranceway. She is carrying a look-alike "Bette" doll, with matching white dress, black and white striped stockings, black Mary Jane shoes, blonde curly hair, and sunglasses. They each hold a cigarette.*)

BETTE. Who the hell is making all the ruckus? We couldn't even finish our cigarettes on the beach.

HATTIE. It's Sister Mae.

TALLULAH. Someone made molehills out of her mountains.

BETTE. What?! Are you sure?

KATHARINE. Sister Bette, I'll have you know that I was an army nurse for ten years in...

(**TALLULAH** *clears her throat threateningly.*)

...a city somewhere in Eastern Pennsylvania, and I've never seen a person who plays a corpse as well as this one.

(**VIVIEN** *re-enters from kitchen hallway.* **BETTE** *sets doll down on the floor behind the sofa.*)

JOAN. We've got to find out who's behind all this.

VIVIEN. Well, whoever it is, they done copped my "Yankee Killer." I can't find it noplace, nohow, nowhere.

(**HATTIE** *pulls up her skirt to reveal an empty leg holster.*)

TALLULAH. The answer's simple, dahlings. It must be Mother Paramount.

BETTE. So why's she doing this? Why won't she show her face?

TALLULAH. But she has, dahling.

KATHARINE. You mean...that Mother Paramount is one of us?

(*They all gasp and ad-lib disbelief.*)

Calm down, everyone. First things, first. Sisters, will someone help me move poor Sister Mae's supple, pouting carcass?

(**VIVIEN** *exits out kitchen hallway.*)

JOAN. Help her, Bette. After all, you've become so adept at *carrying* dead weight.

(**BETTE** *drops her cigarette on the floor and grinds it out with her foot.*)

BETTE. *(to* **JOAN***)* You mean, *pushing* dead weight, don't ya?

(**VIVIEN** *enters from the kitchen hallway carrying the flat furniture dolly with four casters.*)

VIVIEN. Here's the "dead diva dolly."

(*VIVIEN snaps her fingers at* **HATTIE** *ordering her to help.* **HATTIE** *crosses to* **VIVIEN**, *snatches the dolly away from her and snaps her fingers back in* **VIVIEN***'s face.*)

KATHARINE. (*affectionately*) Now come along, Sister Bette. I know that underneath that gruff exterior, you really are a lovable old poop. Now help me here.

(**HATTIE** *and* **BETTE** *lay the dolly on the floor next to* **MAE** *and roll her on top of it.*)

Let's just roll her over, very carefully.

(*They roll the dolly with* **MAE** *lying on top and cross to the kitchen hallway followed by* **KATHARINE**. *During all this, they ad-lib.*)

HATTIE. Poor thing…Don't show all her business!

TALLULAH. I thought showing her business, was her business. Is she awfully heavy? Maybe you should pop her hips too.

BETTE. It's not her; it's that cheap jewelry.

(*They take her part way out the kitchen hallway.*)

(**MARILYN** *picks up the poem and reads it to herself.*)

HATTIE. I've got dibs on her pumps.

KATHARINE. Now Sisters, gently, gently, down the cellar stairs one step at a time.

BETTE. Oops.

(**BETTE** *shoves* **MAE***'s body. There is the sound of* **MAE***'s **body falling down the cellar stairs**. The three Sisters bounce their heads in time to the bumps. There is a pause and then one final, loud thud. All grimace except for* **BETTE**, *who smiles malevolently.*)

TALLULAH. (*referring to Mae*) Down the hatch.

MARILYN. *(referring to the poem)* Listen, listen. I think I see a connection.

VIVIEN. Not.

MARILYN. *(reading aloud)* 'Ten Sisters of San Andreas playing with a vine,
one went and hung herself...

*(She points to the window where **JUDY**'s body was discovered.)*

and then there were nine.'
'Nine Sisters of San Andreas all playing with fate,
one went for bust...

*(She points to the floor where **MAE**'s body was discovered.)*

and then there were eight.'

JOAN. Don't you see? She's killing us off according to that poem.

*(**TALLULAH** points to the nun ring.)*

TALLULAH. Two dead, two fallen. My Gawd, it's a score-card!

KATHARINE. Sister Marilyn, what's the next line of that poem?

MARILYN. *(reading aloud)* 'Eight Sisters of San Andreas aiming for heaven,
one became a centerfold and then...

(She stops reading, mouths the words she has just spoken, and then gasps.)

I must be next!

*(All gasp and take a step away from **MARILYN** who places the poem on the bar.)*

(crying) It's true. It's true. But it's not as bad as it seems. It was when I was a teenager, a time when I was very broke. I know you're not going to believe this, but once I did a dumb thing. I...

MARILYN. *(cont.)* well, I…I exposed my *seven year itch* in public. (**ALL** *adlib gasps, "ewww's" or expressions of disgust*)

BETTE. Well, there goes my appetite.

KATHARINE. I, too, am guilty as charged. I've been shooting loons out of season for years. Once I shot *a lion in winter*. And heaven knows Sister Tallulah indulges in the demons of alcohol.

TALLULAH. Rumor monger.

KATHARINE. Let's face it, Sisters. Mother Paramount has found out that we all have skeletons in our closets and she's about to rattle those bones.

(GLORIA stands and begins to sing and sway.)

GLORIA. Dem bones, dem bones, dem dry bones. Dem bones, dem bones, dem…

VIVIEN. Somebody stuff a sock in this schizo.

(VIVIEN hits GLORIA on the head with her fan. GLORIA sinks into the sofa, indignant.)

This is all poppycock. I'd never ruin anyone else for my own personal gain.

(HATTIE picks up her feet one at a time as if walking through mud.)

HATTIE. It's getting mighty thick in here.

(VIVIEN glares at HATTIE, who sits on stage right bar stool.)

(TALLULAH leaves bar and crosses behind MARILYN to sofa.)

MARILYN. Stop it, all of you! Can't you see I'm next? Which one of you Sisters is doing me tonight?

(TALLULAH does a take towards MARILYN.)

TALLULAH. Would you care to rephrase that, dahling?

(TALLULAH crosses to sofa, sits next to GLORIA, picks up a book entitled "Boozin' With Tallulah," and begins to read.)

MARILYN. *(worried)* What are we going to do, Sister Katharine?

KATHARINE. As long as we remain in this room we will be able to monitor each other's movements. In that way, the murderess, whichever one of us she is, will not have the opportunity to strike.

VIVIEN. Oh, fiddle-dee-dee. This is ridiculous. Mother Paramount is so mean and hateful. She shows no breeding whatsoever, subjecting me to this horrible game of cat-and-mouse. I deserve better. Doesn't she realize what I've done for this organization? And for what? To be reduced to nothing more than a common victim. *(VIVIEN indicates floor where MAE died and window where JUDY and TOTO were discovered hanging from tree.)* Well, I won't put up with it.

(VIVIEN drops to her knees and plunges her hand into the planter. She grabs the trunk of the small palm tree, pulls it out of the dirt and holds it up to the heavens.)

(building in intensity)

As God is my witness…as God is my witness, she's not going to lick me! I'm going to live through this and when it's all over, I'll never be terrorized by her again. Even if I have to lie, steal, cheat…

(harshly)

…or kill the bitch myself. As God…

(snidely and aside)

…and these trashy little tarts…

(back to speech)

…are my witnesses…

(intensely)

…I'll never be *Tara*-ized again.

(All Sisters clap.)

TALLULAH. Brava, dahling. Marvelous speech, marvel-ous.

MARILYN. Yes, inspiring. I almost gave you a standing *ovulation.*

*(**VIVIEN** replaces the plant.)*

VIVIEN. Dumb blonde!

MARILYN. *(to **VIVIEN**, indignant)* Hey! Who are you call-ing 'blonde?'

*(**JOAN** wheels to the bar. **BETTE** follows her, and then crosses behind the bar where she begins to make a cocktail for herself.)*

JOAN. Sisters. Sisters. If we're going to be confined in this room for the duration, perhaps we should do something that will take our minds off our situa-tion.

KATHARINE. Like what?

JOAN. Maybe a nice game of *Clue?*

*(All glare at **JOAN**.)*

Okay...don't get your habits in a knot. Perhaps a nice card game would calm our nerves.

KATHARINE. Excellent idea.

*(Before **BETTE** has the chance to take a sip, **KATHA-RINE** takes the drink from **BETTE** and clutches it in her shaking hand.)*

Why, thank you, bartendress. And don't bother, I'll mix it myself.

*(**KATHARINE** begins to sip her drink as **BETTE** pours another drink for herself and crosses behind the sofa. **BETTE** sits on the stage left arm of the sofa.)*

HATTIE. So, are we gonna play cards or are we gonna sit here and flap our lips?

JOAN. Well, what shall we play?

(KATHARINE pulls a dealer's visor from behind the bar and puts it on her head. She also pulls out a deck of cards and begins to shuffle like a pro.)

KATHARINE. Draw Poker. Jacks or better to open, trips to win, night baseball with a chance of rain, high spade in the hole wins half the pot.

HATTIE. *(snaps at KATHARINE)* Hold on Miss Bobble-Head! I ain't no spade and I don't smoke pot...

MARILYN. *(interrupting)* How about Bridge?

JOAN. No...Gin.

(TALLULAH raises the glass in her hand.)

TALLULAH. Better yet...vodka, dahling!

KATHARINE. *(suggesting card game)* Blackjack!

HATTIE. *(snapping back)* White trash!

KATHARINE. *(exasperated)* Not you...the card game.

(KATHARINE begins to deal cards to MARILYN, HATTIE and herself.)

Kate's my name and dealing's my game. Minimum bet's, a quarter, sawbuck limit. Dealer stands on seventeen, double down on ten or eleven, I'll split any pair.

(VIVIEN paces to center stage.)

VIVIEN. We've got no time for this nonsense.

(They all stop what they're doing and look at her.)

There's a heap of work still to do.

(They all ignore her and return to what each was doing.)

(to herself) I should never have fired our butler... Rhett.

MARILYN. *(referring to cards)* Yoo hoo, Sister Kate. Hit me.

(**KATHARINE** *slaps* **MARILYN** *across the face.*)

MARILYN. *(cont.)* Ow. Not so hard.

KATHARINE. Oh, I'm sorry. I'm overwrought. I don't know what I'm doing.

HATTIE. Are we gonna play cards, or not?

(**MARILYN** *holds her jaw.*)

MARILYN. I don't think I can. I feel a little woozy.

KATHARINE. Perhaps you should lie down in your room for a while.

MARILYN. Do you think its safe, Sister Katharine?

(**KATHARINE** *and* **MARILYN** *cross to bedroom hallway.*)

KATHARINE. Don't worry. We'll all stay right here. Now, when you get to your bedroom, remember to lock the door behind you.

MARILYN. *(faces* **KATHARINE***)* Of course I'll lock the door behind me. If I locked it in front of me, I couldn't get in, silly.

(**MARILYN** *exits to bedroom hallway.*)

JOAN. Bette, since you're just sitting there, denting the furniture, why don't you go into the kitchen and make us some breakfast?

BETTE. Why should I make breakfast? That's Sister Hattie's job.

HATTIE. Wait a minute, little Miss Bug Eyes. Where is it written that the large, sexy black woman always has to do the cooking around here?

JOAN. *(begging)* Oh, please, you must! I'm so hungry!

HATTIE. *(mimicking Joan)* Of course you're hungry.

(mimicking Bette)

'Cuz you didn't eat your din-din.'

*(A loud "sproing" is heard as a **Murphy Bed crashes into the wall**. We hear a piercing scream*

from offstage. All panic and ad-lib as they rush out to the bedroom hallway leaving **JOAN** *onstage. The sound of a fist pounding on a door is heard off-stage.)*

BETTE. *(offstage)* It's locked!

JOAN. *(shouting down the hallway)* You've got to get in there! Find some heavy and expendable object to break the door in!

TALLULAH. *(offstage)* Here's something nobody will miss.

BETTE. *(offstage)* What the hell are you looking at?

TALLULAH. *(offstage)* You, dahling!

BETTE. *(offstage)* Oh, *no* you don't!

(**BETTE** *rushes out on stage followed quickly by* **KATHARINE**, **HATTIE** *and* **TALLULAH**. *They catch her and pick her up as if she was a battering ram.* **VIVIEN** *"directs" them towards the door and they "charge" off stage. We hear a thud as* **BETTE**'s *head "hits" the offstage door. While still carrying* **BETTE**; **KATHARINE**, **HATTIE** *and* **TALLULAH** *rush back onstage and repeat the battering ram motion. We hear another thud as* **BETTE**'s *head "hits" the off-stage door once again. The entire action is repeated a third time. We then hear the sound of a **door crashing in** and All [except* **JOAN**] *exit completely off stage.)*

VIVIEN. *(offstage)* Sister Marilyn!

JOAN. *(shouting down the hallway)* Quick, pull the Murphy bed down!

(Screams are heard off stage.)

How horrible! Goodbye, Norma Jean.

*(As the lights fade, **The Hand Sting with The Witch's Cackle and Mystery Track (spooky)** is heard. A spot light comes up on the Mother*

*Paramount portrait. A black-gloved hand opens the portrait and tips over a nun figurine. The action should be timed so that **The Witch's Cackle** is heard as the portrait is closed. The spot light fades to Blackout and the **Mystery Track (spooky)** continues to play.)*

Scene Two

*(The time is early that same evening. All remaining Sisters enter during Blackout. As the lights come up, the **Mystery Track (spooky)** fades out. **BETTE** is seated on a barstool. **GLORIA** is standing on the edge of the bottom balcony stair as if she were about to jump. **KATHARINE** and **HATTIE** are seated on the sofa. **VIVIEN** is seated on the stage right arm of the sofa. **BETTE, GLORIA, KATHARINE, HATTIE** and **VIVIEN** have their heads bowed as in prayer. **TALLULAH** is hidden behind the bar. **JOAN** wheels in next to the Victrola placing a silver tray with three lit votive candles on top of it. The stage lights come up.)*

JOAN. I've lit candles for our fallen Sisters.

VIVIEN. Wasn't it ghastly how those horrible spikes in the wall impaled her?

HATTIE. Just like a giant staple...right through her belly...

KATHARINE. *(interrupting, referring to poem)* Wait a minute. 'One became a centerfold and then there were seven.' Talk about a perfectionist. Paramount must be a damn Virgo...

HATTIE. *(interrupting)* ...or very anal-retentive.

VIVIEN. I still don't understand how that Murphy bed could flip up with Sister Marilyn laying on it.

KATHARINE. Obviously, Mother Paramount is a whiz with a screwdriver.

*(**TALLULAH** pops up from behind the bar holding a bottle of vodka. She slams the bottle on the bar.)*

TALLULAH. Screwdriver? Don't mind if I do.

GLORIA. *Heathcliff,* I can't bear life any longer!

*(All the Sisters look at **GLORIA**.)*

GLORIA. *(cont.)* I've seen the vultures circling above the *moors*, Dudley and Mary Tyler. That's why you must learn to love another for tomorrow I shall be buried deep in the mire. Shall I jump now, Sister DeMille? Thank you.

(GLORIA jumps the short distance from the bottom step to the floor. Immediately the other Sisters hold up scoring cards, i.e., 5.2, 5.4, etc. BETTE holds up cards with "0.0.")

BETTE. Big deal!

TALLULAH. Lousy form.

VIVIEN. Her feet didn't stay together.

GLORIA. I would have scored higher but the sun was in my eyes...

KATHARINE. Obviously, she's been deprived of oxygen for several decades.

BETTE. Sister Tallulah, what are the next lines in our ode to eternal fame?

TALLULAH. *(reading aloud)* 'Seven Sisters of San Andreas acting in the flicks,

One's career got cut, and then there were six.'

HATTIE. That's it! I'm not waitin' around for someone to chop me into stew meat! I'm going to lock myself in my room. If any of you porkers get hungry, you can fend for yourselves.

(HATTIE hurries out to bedroom hallway.)

KATHARINE. In her usual understated way, Sister Hattie has the right idea. I think what we all need to do is meditate and ask for guidance. I suggest we forego our services this evening and spend the time locked safely in our rooms.

TALLULAH. What? And end up like Sister Marilyn... plastered against the wall.

BETTE. *(to TALLULAH)* Something you're not unfamiliar with.

(**KATHARINE** *rises and puts her hands together as if in prayer. She leaves her handbag on the sofa. The remaining Sisters, with the exception of* **TALLU-LAH** *[drinking at the bar] bow their heads, praying under their breath; form a line across the stage.*)

KATHARINE. Sister Tallulah, will you haul it on down here!

TALLULAH. I'm hauling.

(**TALLULAH** *joins the other Sisters in line.*)

(*under her breath*)

The brochure said "Fun in the Sun." That's the last time I trust a travel agent named Hitchcock.

KATHARINE. Will you shut up?! Sisters, are you ready?

(*They all stop praying and swing their right arms outward.*)

ALL. (*ala Curly Howard*) S-oy-tenly! Woo-woo-woo, woo-woo-woo!

(*They suddenly break into a two-hand finger snap and skip. As they exit out bedroom hallway, heads bowed, they all chant the MGM motto.*)

ALL. Ars, Gratia, Artis. Ars, Gratia, Artis.

(**BETTE** *is the last Sister to leave. As she gets to the Victrola, she blows out the three votive candles.*)

BETTE. A-men!

(**BETTE** *exits. The* **Mystery Track (spooky)** *plays. The lights dim as we hear* **doors shutting and locking**. *The 8' tall gold statue slowly swings open and* **HATTIE** *enters from the secret passageway. The* **Mystery Track (spooky)** *fades out.*)

HATTIE. Those Sisters can play games if they want to. Sister Hattie ain't gonna be a guinea pig for nobody. I know who the murderess is and I'm gonna get her before she gets me. Now where did that crazy blonde hide that knife?

(**HATTIE** *creeps to the closet. We hear* **Psycho-ee Music** *start to play.* **HATTIE** *draws back the outer curtain and enters the closet stepping behind an inner shower curtain. She pulls on the light cord, which turns on a bare bulb, casting her shadow on the inner curtain.*)

(*Suddenly from behind her, a cloaked assailant appears inside the closet. The cloaked assailant repeatedly brings a knife up and down as* **HATTIE** *screams while being stabbed. The* **Psycho-ee Music** *fades out as* **HATTIE** *slumps to the floor.* **HATTIE** *pulls the shower curtain down with her. The assailant turns off the closet light. A spot light comes up on the Mother Paramount portrait. We hear* **The Hand Sting with The Witch's Cackle** *as the black-gloved hand opens the portrait and tips over a nun figurine. The action should be timed so that* **The Witch's Cackle** *is heard as the portrait is closed. The spot light fades out as* **VIVIEN** *enters from the bedroom hallway and switches on the lights.*)

VIVIEN. Who's out there? What was that noise? Sister Hattie is that you? Sister Hattie?

(**KATHARINE** *enters from the bedroom hallway.*)

KATHARINE. Oh, Sister Vivien, have you seen my handbag? I know I left it here someplace.

VIVIEN. (*under her breath*) Yes. It's probably in Philadelphia.

KATHARINE. Oh, here it is.

(**KATHARINE** *picks up her handbag from the sofa just as* **VIVIEN** *discovers* **HATTIE**'s *body.*)

(**VIVIEN** *screams which makes* **KATHARINE** *jump. She turns to* **VIVIEN** *and indicates her handbag.*)

(*flustered*) Well, it's not Louis Vuiton, but it's the best I have!

(All remaining Sisters enter. **JOAN** *has the birdcage on her lap.* **VIVIEN** *begins a high-pitched cry.)*

VIVIEN. Not my hefty Hattie.

KATHARINE. *(running to* **HATTIE***)* Oh, no. Not *the African queen!*

VIVIEN. *(grief-stricken)* Who's going to wax my floors? Who's going to wax my car?

(aside)

Who's going to wax my moustache?

GLORIA. *(to* **VIVIEN***)* There, there, Sister Vivien. She was a good little soldier.

VIVIEN. I can't help it. She was my best friend.

GLORIA. *(takes a beat)* She was your only friend.

(to audience)

Well, she was...

VIVIEN. There's no use in going on anymore.

(cries again)

GLORIA. *(seemingly sane)* Oh, yes there is, my child. You and I have everything to live for.

VIVIEN. *(tries to stop crying)* Like what?

GLORIA. Well...we've got days that are sunny with never a care...we've got our Sisters who are chipper all the day. I've got Him up above and you here below...and...

(GLORIA *pulls open her skirt, the inside of which is now lined with an American Flag. She begins to march while singing "I'm A Yankee Doodle Dandy.")*

(singing)

'I'm a Yankee Doodle Dandy.

A Yankee Doodle, do or die.'

VIVIEN. I'll kill this crazy yank!

(**VIVIEN** *swings around and pounces on* **GLORIA** *and starts to strangle her.*)

KATHARINE. Somebody stop them! Get a grip.

(**KATHARINE** *rushes in the middle and separates* **VIVIEN** *and* **GLORIA.**)

(**BETTE** *grabs* **VIVIEN** *and shoves her down on the sofa.* **TALLULAH** *holds back* **GLORIA.**)

BETTE. *(to* **VIVIEN***)* You're acting as crazy as she is.

TALLULAH. *(to* **GLORIA***)* Retreat, Sister Gloria, retreat. To the tower, quickly.

(**TALLULAH** *points to the stairs.* **GLORIA** *taps* **KATHARINE** *on both shoulders with an imaginary sword.*)

GLORIA. I dub thee Sir Shake of Bake, *Knight of the Iguana.*

(**GLORIA** *ascends the stairs and exits out the front entranceway.* **TALLULAH** *crosses to* **HATTIE.**)

TALLULAH. Will someone help me with this debris? She's wreaking havoc with the decor.

(**GLORIA** *re-enters through the front entranceway carrying the furniture dolly.*)

GLORIA. *(ala Carol Channing)* Well, *hello, dolly.*

(**GLORIA** *places the dolly on the floor next to* **HATTIE.**)

KATHARINE. Could you help, Sister Bette?

(**GLORIA** *and* **TALLULAH** *roll* **HATTIE** *onto the dolly.*)

JOAN. Yes, Bette.

BETTE. *(irritated)* Gee, I should have volunteered.

TALLULAH. Thank you so much.

(**BETTE** *covers* **HATTIE** *with the shower curtain.*)

BETTE. I guess its *curtains* for Sister Hattie.

(BETTE, TALLULAH and GLORIA start to pull and/or push HATTIE on the dolly towards the kitchen hallway.)

GLORIA. I suggest putting her in the pool.

TALLULAH. Wouldn't she clog the drain?

(They continue to ad-lib as they finish their cross to the kitchen hallway.)

Let's put her in the cellar. Some of my best friends are in the cellar.

BETTE. They must be rats.

TALLULAH. *(to BETTE)* I'd love to meet *your* family.

(They roll HATTIE part way out the kitchen doorway followed by KATHARINE.)

KATHARINE. Gently, gently, now. One step at a time.

BETTE. Aw, just push her.

*(BETTE tilts the dolly and we hear HATTIE's **body falling down the cellar stairs**. Their heads bounce in cadence to the rhythmic thumps as her body "hits" each stair.)*

(BETTE, TALLULAH and GLORIA re-enter and gather around the bar.)

(KATHARINE picks up the poem.)

BETTE. Now hear this! There are no more vacancies in the deep freeze.

(JOAN wheels over next to the bar and places the birdcage on an empty bar stool.)

JOAN. I don't know about you girls, but I need a stiff one.

TALLULAH. There are several in the cellar, dahling. Take your pick!

JOAN. I shouldn't on an empty stomach, but fill 'er up.

(VIVIEN crosses behind the bar between KATHARINE and TALLULAH.)

VIVIEN. Me, too.

> (**TALLULAH** *pours a drink for* **JOAN** *and* **VIVIEN**.)

KATHARINE. *(reading aloud)* 'Six Sisters of San Andreas playing near a hive,
One got stung, and then there were five.
Five Sisters of San Andreas finding one a bore,
They locked her in a closet, and then there were four.'

VIVIEN. *(to* **KATHARINE***)* I think you have dibs on that last death, Sister.

JOAN. *(fainting)* Oh-h-h-h.

> (**KATHARINE** *drops poem on the bar and rushes over to* **JOAN**)

KATHARINE. Sister Joan! Sister Joan!

> (**BETTE** *pushes* **KATHARINE** *aside*.)

BETTE. *(to* **KATHARINE***)* Here, let *me* handle this.

> (**BETTE** *faces* **JOAN**. *Her back is to the audience.*)

Joan! Wake up, Joan!

> (**BETTE** *slaps* **JOAN**'s *face twice.*)

> (**JOAN** *comes to and slaps* **BETTE** *across the face.*)

> (**BETTE** *staggers away.*)

JOAN. Oh, Bette, I didn't know it was you.

> *(Takes a beat. Then, sarcastically)*

Really.

> *(back to normal)*

I thought you were...Christina. What happened?

KATHARINE. You fainted dear.

TALLULAH. Passed out is more like it.

JOAN. I guess I shouldn't drink so much on an *empty* stomach.

TALLULAH. Why not? I always do.

KATHARINE. Perhaps a bit of nourishment would do us all some good. Sister Bette, would you be so kind as to help me in the kitchen?

(**KATHARINE** *exits to kitchen hallway.*)

JOAN. Oh, would you, sister dear?

BETTE. (*imitating* **JOAN**) Oh, would you, sister dear? Don't worry, sister dearest. I'll make sure you and your precious Pookie get what you deserve.

(**JOAN** *picks up the birdcage and hands it to* **BETTE.**)

JOAN. Oh, thank you! And would you clean his cage, too?

BETTE. It's what I live for.

(**BETTE** *grabs the birdcage and slings it over her shoulder. She exits to kitchen hallway.*)

JOAN. Oh, bless you Sister. Bless you.

VIVIEN. (*to* **TALLULAH**) Sister Tallulah?

TALLULAH. What?

(**VIVIEN** *tries unsuccessfully to sit on a bar stool with her hoop skirt. Finally, she lifts up the hoop skirt, tip toes over the bar stool, drops the skirt over the stool, hops the chair to the bar, and then sits.*)

TALLULAH. (*cont.*) I'm impressed.

VIVIEN. Sister Tallulah, I know I haven't been the easiest person to get along with, but...

(**GLORIA, TALLULAH** *and* **JOAN** *begin to hum the chorus of "The Battle Hymn of the Republic" in the background.*)

...everything I've done, I've done for the prosperity of the Order...for the good of my fellow Sisters...

(*building in intensity*)

...for the sanctity of the motion picture screen, and for the glory of my beloved South!

GLORIA, TALLULAH & JOAN. (*still in tune with song*) ...
The tramp keeps rambling on!

(**BETTE** *enters from kitchen hallway carrying two
Swanson frozen TV dinners in their original pack-
aging and a bunch of fake grapes.*)

BETTE. Here's your din-din.

(**BETTE** *tosses a TV dinner to* **VIVIEN** *and* **TALLU-
LAH** *who catch them.*)

(*to* **TALLULAH**)

Sister T. You better eat it quickly or I'll take all your
best parts. Wait. I already did!

(*Ala Mae West*)

Oh, Buella...peel me a grape.

(*She tosses the bunch of fake grapes to* **GLORIA** *over*
JOAN's *head who tries to intercept it.* **GLORIA** *ravenously "eats" the grapes.*)

JOAN. (*indicating* **GLORIA**) But Bette, shouldn't she have
gotten a *Swanson* dinner too? And where's mine?

BETTE. (*ominously sweet*) Don't worry, sister. You'll get
what's coming to you.

(**BETTE** *exits back out kitchen hallway.*)

(*From the kitchen, we hear the sound of a* **blender**.)

(**JOAN** *repeatedly presses her buzzer.*)

JOAN. (*demanding*) Bette, where's my dinner?

(*The* **blender** *stops.* **BETTE** *enters carrying a tray in
one hand. On the tray is a Shredded Wheat cereal
box and a bowl. In her other hand she is carrying
the now-empty birdcage.*)

BETTE. (*shouting*) Stop with the frigging buzzer!

(**JOAN** *stops pressing the buzzer.*)

Here's your dinner.

(**BETTE** *places the tray on* **JOAN**'s *lap.*)

Oh, by the way. I lined the bottom of the cage with one of your pictures.

(**BETTE** *tilts the birdcage to show* **JOAN** *[and the audience] an 8 x 10 picture of* **JOAN** *taped to the bottom of the cage.*)

Now the bird can do to ya what all your friends do to ya.

JOAN. But where's Pookie?

BETTE. He got out.

(**GLORIA** *surveys the ceiling looking for Pookie.*)

JOAN. *(surprised)* He did?! Where did he go?!

BETTE. I don't know. He disappeared when I turned on the Mixmaster. Don't worry. He'll be back. Now eat your din-din before it gets cold.

JOAN. What am I having?

(**BETTE** *picks up the Shredded Wheat cereal box with an ominous look, opens it, and dumps out many feathers which match the color of Pookie.*)

BETTE. ...shredded *tweet*!

(**JOAN** *screams as* **BETTE** *laughs and throws the box in the air.* **BETTE** *exits out the kitchen hallway.*)

(**GLORIA** *grabs the Shredded Wheat box and starts to pick up the feathers from the floor, shoving them back into the box.*)

(**VIVIEN** *rushes out bedroom hallway covering her mouth as though she were going to be sick.* **JOAN** *puts her tray on the bar and wheels after* **VIVIEN**.)

JOAN. Sister Vivien, Sister Vivien, it's just Bette's warped sense of humor. She would never hurt Pookie.

(**JOAN** *exits to bedroom hallway.*)

TALLULAH. *(laughing)* I just love this place.

(to the portrait of Mother Paramount)

Thanks for inviting me, dahling!

(GLORIA *continues to pick up the feathers then motions to* **TALLULAH.** *)*

GLORIA. *(to* **TALLULAH***)* You there, Corporal…

(ala Paul Revere's ride)

Come hither and you shall hear about a midnight plot I've engineered.

(GLORIA *rises and puts her arm around* **TALLULAH***'s shoulder. As they ascend the stairs to the balcony by the front entranceway,* **GLORIA** *is whispering in* **TALLULAH***'s ear and gesturing broadly.)*

(BETTE *enters from kitchen hallway "dusting" the air with a feather duster. The duster is obviously missing some feathers.* **KATHARINE** *picks up a feather from the floor and holds it up to the feather duster. She realizes that they are a perfect match.)*

KATHARINE. *(to* **BETTE***)* Sister, you are a mental case!

(JOAN *enters from the bedroom hallway pressing her buzzer. She crosses to* **BETTE.** *)*

JOAN. Bette! How could you be so cruel?!

(JOAN *continues to press her buzzer.)*

BETTE. *(agitated)* Quiet! Now, I'm going to take care of that frigging buzzer!

(BETTE *grabs the buzzer. We hear **electric sparks** as* **BETTE** *is electrocuted.)*

(Simultaneously, **TALLULAH** *flickers the light switch and then turns them off creating a complete Blackout.)*

JOAN. Bette! Bette! Where are you?

(**VIVIEN** *enters into the dark from the bedroom hall-way.*)

VIVIEN. What happened? Who turned out the lights?

KATHARINE. Somebody find a match.

TALLULAH. Sister Gloria, where are you?

(**TALLULAH** *lights a cigarette lighter in front of* **GLORIA**'s *face.*)

GLORIA. Happy birthday to me.

(**GLORIA** *blows out the flame.*)

(***The Witch's Cackle*** *is heard.*)

VIVIEN. Who is that laughing?

(*Two loud thumping noises are heard.*)

(**VIVIEN** *lights a cigarette lighter and holds it in front of her face.*)

What was that noise?

(**VIVIEN**'s *lighter goes out.* **KATHARINE** *lights a cigarette lighter.*)

KATHARINE. This reminds me of a blackout we had in Phila...

(**KATHARINE**'s *finger is burned by the cigarette lighter.*)

...ouch!

(*The cigarette lighter goes out. In the darkness,* **KATHARINE** *exits*)

JOAN. Bette, Bette. Where are you?

(*Two more loud thumping noises are heard.*)

My God, what did I just run over?

KATHARINE. *(at kitchen hallway)* I found the light switch.

(**KATHARINE** *switches on the light switch and immediately the lights come back on.*)

(**GLORIA** *is standing motionless in a clear garment bag in the closet.*)

(**BETTE** *is lying on the floor.*)

TALLULAH. *(reacting to Bette's body)* Oh, my Gawd!

JOAN. It's Bette!

(**VIVIEN** *points toward* **GLORIA**.)

VIVIEN. And looney tunes, too!

(**TALLULAH** *crosses to* **GLORIA** *in the closet.*)

KATHARINE. Now I know what they mean by a "Blue Nun."

TALLULAH. All right. Which one of you broads martinized Sister Gloria?

(**TALLULAH** *snaps the closet curtain closed.*)

JOAN. *(angrily)* Who cares about her?

(melodramatically)

Look what someone did to my poor, lovable baby sister. Who's going to oil my wheelchair? Who's going to fix my din-din? Who's going to chain me to my bed and make me watch old Ronald Reagan movies?

TALLULAH. You're not fooling anyone with that maudlin crap.

VIVIEN. Yeah! It was your chair that blew her pilot light out. And would you mind telling me what these tire tracks are doing all over her rather spindly cadaver?

JOAN. I...I...I...didn't see her. It was dark.

(**VIVIEN** *counts several lines on the body.*)

VIVIEN. Well, it appears you didn't see her several times.

KATHARINE. Stop it, Sisters! Stop it! This caterwauling is getting us nowhere. We have to pull ourselves up by our chinstraps. Sister Tallulah, help me with Sister Bette and Sister Vivien, you go get Squirrelly Shirley off the rack.

VIVIEN. I couldn't...I can't...I won't...and you can't make me.

(**KATHARINE** *crosses toward* **VIVIEN** *threateningly.*)

KATHARINE. Look, Little Miss Muffet...you've been sitting on that antebellum tuffet of yours all weekend while I've spent the last two days watching my fellow Sisters buy the farm. I'm tired...I'm cranky...I have *PMS*...so don't you f...f...f...fiddle-dee-dee with me.

VIVIEN. (*to* JOAN *while pointing at* KATHARINE) She's power hungry I tell you. A trait not uncommon in cold-blooded murderers.

KATHARINE. Who do you think you're calling cold-blooded, you vindictive little viper?

(*Mumbling,* **TALLULAH** *crosses to* **BETTE** *and tries to pick her up by herself.*)

(*indicating* JOAN) And anyway, you're probably in on this whole thing with Miss Wheels.

JOAN. (*indicating* VIVIEN) I would never debauch my reputation by conspiring with rebel slime.

VIVIEN. (*screeching*) Slime!?

(**TALLULAH** *falters as she tries to pick up* **BETTE**.)

TALLULAH. I can't pick up this old woman. She's as big as a *lifeboat*. Can't we just cut her up a bit?

KATHARINE. Enough of this nonsense.

(*to* VIVIEN)

I'll deal with you later.

(*to* TALLULAH)

Here, let me help you.

(TALLULAH holds up one of BETTE's legs.)

TALLULAH. *(referring to Bette's striped stockings)* We could stand her in front of a barbershop.

KATHARINE. No dear, she'd scare away the customers.

TALLULAH. At least she'd be working.

(With great effort, TALLULAH and KATHARINE pick up BETTE and carry her backwards towards JOAN.)

(JOAN repeatedly presses her buzzer imitating the backup-warning sounds of a large truck.)

JOAN. Back her up girls. That's it. Bring the load back.

(They drop BETTE in JOAN's lap. JOAN reacts to the weight of BETTE and stops pressing the buzzer. KATHARINE crosses to kitchen hallway. TALLULAH pushes JOAN (and BETTE) in wheelchair.)

Oh my God, she is heavy!

TALLULAH. Say, is there anything in that poem about being crushed to death?

KATHARINE. Not that I remember.

(TALLULAH pushes JOAN's wheelchair with JOAN and BETTE halfway out the kitchen hallway.)

TALLULAH. This is as far as I go.

JOAN. Well, you don't expect me to go down those stairs in this wheelchair, do you?

TALLULAH. Fine, then. Jump, Bette, jump!

*(TALLULAH pushes BETTE's body out of the wheelchair. We hear BETTE's **body falling down the cellar stairs**. They again follow the "thumps" with their heads.)*

Oh...what's black and white, black and white, black and white...and...oh, black and **blue**.

(**TALLULAH** *reenters brushing her hands off, followed by* **KATHARINE**. *An irritated* **JOAN** *wheels in after them.*)

TALLULAH. *(cont.)* Sister Bette had to take a sudden little trip down south. Too bad she didn't have time to pack.

JOAN. You wicked old woman! Bette would have kicked your butt, if she wasn't already dead.

(**TALLULAH** *moves to the bar imitating* **BETTE** *in voice and exaggerated mannerisms.*)

TALLULAH. But she *is* dead, Sister, she is. And I think you killed her.

JOAN. How dare you accuse me, you over-lubricated, antiquity?! I could never be Mother Paramount. She's obviously a tough, diabolical, clever, sarcastic woman who has been influenced by the effects of over-indulgence in alcohol and Scientology.

(*All slowly turn their heads towards* **TALLULAH** *who is unaware that they are staring at her.*)

TALLULAH. *(clueless, reading aloud)* 'Four Sisters of San Andreas amid a murderer's spree...'

(**TALLULAH** *abruptly stops and turns to the others who are staring at her.*)

What the hell are you looking at?

(*In unison they all look away.*)

'...One's chalice was poisoned...'

(**TALLULAH** *takes a drink from her glass and continues reading.*)

...and then there were three.'

(**TALLULAH** *stops. Looks at her glass. Does a take to the audience.*)

Uh, oh.

(**TALLULAH** *immediately collapses over the bar.*)

KATHARINE. Not again.

(**KATHARINE** *crosses to her and feels her pulse.*)

JOAN. Is she..?

VIVIEN. ...dead?

KATHARINE. Yes, she's dead all right...dead drunk.

(**KATHARINE** *lifts* **TALLULAH***'s head and looks at her.* **TALLULAH***'s eyes are closed.* **KATHARINE** *drops* **TALLULAH***'s head back onto the bar with a 'thud.'*)

Well, what did you expect? She's been drinking for two acts. Sister Vivien, come over here and help me move the Seagrams' poster child over to the sofa. Sister Joan, go fetch some coffee. Make it black.

JOAN. *(perturbed)* What do I look like...meals on wheels?

KATHARINE. *(exasperated)* Just do it.

(**JOAN** *wheels to the coffee service and pours a cup of coffee.* **KATHARINE,** *with a minimal amount of help from* **VIVIEN,** *drags* **TALLULAH** *to the sofa.*)

(**KATHARINE** *and* **VIVIEN** *stand over* **TALLULAH** *and try to revive her.*)

(**JOAN** *tilts her head sideways, places the handle of the coffee cup in her mouth, and wheels to the others.*)

Come on Sister Tallulah, sober up.

VIVIEN. I think she's coming to. I can see the reds of her eyes.

(**TALLULAH** *suddenly awakens and sees* **VIVIEN** *and* **KATHARINE** *looking over her. She screams.*)

TALLULAH. My Gawd! I've died and gone to hell. I should have known I'd meet you two there.

(**JOAN** *hands the cup of coffee to* **VIVIEN.**)

JOAN. Here's her damn coffee.

(**VIVIEN** *hands the cup of coffee to* **TALLULAH**.)

VIVIEN. Here's your damn coffee.

(**TALLULAH** *hands the cup of coffee to* **KATHA-RINE**.)

TALLULAH. *(to* **KATHARINE***)* Here's your damn coffee.

(**KATHARINE** *hands the cup of coffee back to* **TALLULAH**.)

KATHARINE. *(to* **TALLULAH***)* Here's *your* damn coffee.

(**KATHARINE** *guides the cup to* **TALLULAH***'s mouth.*)

Now drink it all up. Sister Vivien claims her coffee is good to the last drop.

(**TALLULAH** *takes a drink.*)

I hope she didn't make it too strong.

TALLULAH. Just a tad, dahling.

(**TALLULAH** *collapses off the sofa and onto the floor still clutching the coffee cup. Her back is to the audience.*)

JOAN. Oh, no...there she goes again.

(**KATHARINE** *bends over* **TALLULAH**.)

(**VIVIEN** *turns away and begins to check her makeup in her ring-mirror.*)

KATHARINE. Sister Tallulah. Sister Tallulah.

(**KATHARINE** *taps* **TALLULAH***'s cheeks back and forth as:*)

She...is...not...ac-...-know-...-led-...-ging.

JOAN. *(concerned)* Wait a minute, Sister Katharine. Is she breathing?

(**KATHARINE** *looks at* **VIVIEN** *and grabs her hand which has the ring-mirror on it.*)

KATHARINE. Fine time to do your makeup. Give me that.

(**KATHARINE** *places the mirror, still attached to* **VIVIEN**'s *finger, under* **TALLULAH**'s *nose and then examines it.*)

No, she's not.

VIVIEN. *(sarcastically, pulling her hand back)* Pity.

JOAN. Let me see that cup.

(**VIVIEN** *leans down to pick up the cup.*)

(**TALLULAH**'s *hand remains clutched to the handle.*)

VIVIEN. Damn rigor mortis.

(**VIVIEN** *yanks the cup from* **TALLULAH**'s *hand which then falls to the floor with a thud.* **VIVIEN** *shrugs and hands the cup to* **JOAN**.)

(**JOAN** *smells the cup, grimaces, and turns her head away.*)

JOAN. Whew! Wait a minute. Oh my gosh…it's Potassium Cyanide!

(**VIVIEN** *and* **KATHARINE** *gasp.*)

(authoritatively) First discovered in 1882 by Dr. Zazu Pitts in the Cornel Wildes…

(matter-of-factly)

…that's *north by northwest* of Lake Titicaca.

(back to description)

Used by the Fujis, a tribe of Japanese headhunters, as a weapon against enemies, in-laws, and mimes.

KATHARINE. Mimes, oh good, I hate the pasty-faced devils!

JOAN. Three ounces when mixed with a water supply could kill the entire island of Manhattan, and *hopefully*, most of New Jersey.

VIVIEN. *Damn Yankees!*

JOAN. It acts quickly and efficiently and leaves only a slight discoloration about the lips.

(**KATHARINE** and **VIVIEN** *immediately glance at* **TALLULAH**'s *lips and then back up.*)

VIVIEN. *(evil grin)* But is it painful?

JOAN. Can't say. I really don't know that much about it.

KATHARINE. *(accusatory)* Don't know much about it, like hell! You're the one who brought the coffee.

JOAN. But you're the one who gave it to her. You could have easily dropped the poison into the cup.

VIVIEN. Ye–ah.

KATHARINE. *(to* **VIVIEN***)* But you're the one who perked it. Good to the last drop, eh? You mean good until we all drop, don't you? Tired of picking us off one by one? Want to make a clean sweep of it? Well, it won't work, Mother Paramount!

(**VIVIEN** *screams and jumps over* **TALLULAH**'s *body to distance herself from* **KATHARINE***.*)

VIVIEN. I'm not Mother Paramount and I didn't poison nobody, nohow, I tell you...

(pointing to **JOAN***)*

...it's Little Miss Shoulder Pads of Death! She had the most opportune chance to slip her a Minnie.

KATHARINE. That's Mickey, Sister.

VIVIEN. Well, I knew it was one of them Disney mice. But the point remains that such heinous murders could only be perpetrated by a cold, calculating, beady-eyed barbarian. So, if the "come 'F'-me" Pradas fit, wear'em, Sister Joan!

JOAN. *(erupts)* Why, you plantation princess, just wait 'til I get my hands on you!

(**JOAN** *wheels toward* **VIVIEN** *threateningly.*)

VIVIEN. No! No! Help me!

JOAN. *(maniacal)* Bonsai!

(VIVIEN screams and exits to bedroom hallway with JOAN in hot pursuit.)

(KATHARINE leans out bedroom hallway yelling at VIVIEN and JOAN.)

KATHARINE. Sisters, come back here! Sisters! Can you hear me?

(indicating TALLULAH)

You don't expect me to move "Two Tons of Fun" by myself, do you? Sisters, can you hear me? Can you hear..?

(JOAN wheels back in quickly, surprising KATHARINE.)

JOAN. I can hear you. Do what you want with her. I couldn't care less. In the meantime, I'm going to shove those hoops up that Dixiebelle's Mason-Dixon line.

(JOAN exits out bedroom hallway.)

KATHARINE. Well, I never...such rudeness. I tell you Sister Tallulah; such disrespect would never have been tolerated in Phila...

(KATHARINE stops. She looks all around cautiously; then she smiles, leans down and kneels next to TALLULAH.)

(shouting triumphantly)

Philadelphia!

(KATHARINE picks up TALLULAH's hand and pats it as she speaks.)

Did I ever tell you about the time I lived in Philadelphia? No dear, don't get up. Well, Mother and I went to feed the ducks one day and she said to me 'Kate...' she always called me Kate...

*(**KATHARINE** drops **TALLULAH**'s hand.)*

KATHARINE. *(cont.)* What the hell am I doing? I'm the only person alive in this whole room and I've heard this boring story more times than you've had botox. Well, I'll never be able to move you by myself, but I just can't leave you here. At least I could cover you up until morning.

*(She takes **GLORIA**'s coat from the closet and turns toward **TALLULAH**.)*

This should do quite nicely.

(A black-gloved hand appears through the closet curtain and picks up the small statuette on the pedestal near the closet.)

Wait a minute.

*(**KATHARINE** feels something in the pocket of the coat. As she bends over to retrieve it, the black-gloved hand swipes at **KATHARINE**'s head with the statuette, and misses.)*

What's this?

*(**KATHARINE** pulls a gun from the pocket of the coat.)*

Why…it's a revolver. What's it doing here? Whose coat is this anyway?

*(As **KATHARINE** bends over to read the label in the coat, the assailant takes another swing at **KATHARINE**'s head with the statuette, and misses again. The "hand" registers frustration.)*

The label says, 'Sister…' But that's impossible, she's…

(excitedly)

But of course…

*(**KATHARINE** pulls a fake red herring from inside the coat.)*

KATHARINE. *(cont.)* A red herring!

*(**KATHARINE** raises her arm and exclaims:)*

Oh, Sister Tallulah. I know who the murderess is! It's Sister...

*(The assailant brings the statuette down on **KATHA-RINE**'s head, this time with success. The assailant quickly replaces the statuette back on the shelf and grabs the gun from the stunned **KATHARINE**'s hand. **KATHARINE** shakes back and forth as she slowly crosses then falls behind the sofa. She then immediately rises carrying a bouquet of calla lilies.)*

The calla lilies are in bloom again...

*(**KATHARINE** falls again behind the sofa. Her feet end up crossed and resting on the back of the sofa. **The Hand Sting with The Witch's Cackle and Mystery Track (spooky)** is heard.)*

*(As the lights begin to fade, a spot light comes up on the Mother Paramount portrait. A black-gloved hand opens the portrait and tips over four nun figurines. The action should be timed so that **The Witch's Cackle** is heard as the portrait is closed.)*

*(The spot light fades to Blackout and **The Mystery Track (spooky)** continues to play.)*

Scene Three

(The time is the next morning. The bodies of **KATHARINE** *and* **TALLULAH** *remain in the same positions.)*

(The **Mystery Track (spooky)** *fades out as lights come up.* **JOAN** *wheels out from the bedroom hallway and glances at* **TALLULAH**.*)*

JOAN. *(talking to* **TALLULAH***)* Oh, good morning. Almost forgot about you, Shamu. God, I need a Pepsi.

*(***JOAN** *wheels toward the bar and glances up at the china nun ring but stops suddenly.)*

Oh, my! Only two of the china nuns are still standing.

(frightened)

Me...and who else? Let me see that poem.

(She grabs the poem off the bar and reads aloud.)

'Three Sisters of San Andreas discovering a clue, It played heavy on one's mind, and then there were two.'

(She turns her chair and spies **KATHARINE***'s feet.)*

Oh, no! It's Sister Katharine!

(does a take to the audience)

I'd recognize those comfortable shoes anywhere.

*(***VIVIEN** *enters from bedroom hallway.)*

VIVIEN. *(triumphantly to* **JOAN***)* Well, look who has their grubby little digits in the cookie jar. She's dead, isn't she?

JOAN. Yes, she is. But I didn't do it.

VIVIEN. You can't fool me. You're Mother Paramount as sure as I'm the sweet, innocent, and enchanting beauty you see before you.

(**VIVIEN** *produces the "Yankee Killer" from behind her back and points it at* **JOAN**.)

So raise your hands. Your grass is ass.

JOAN. *(registers confusion)* My what, is what?

VIVIEN. Never mind, raise 'em, toots.

JOAN. It's the "Yankee Killer!" You're the one who took it! I know the circumstances appear incriminating, but give me a chance to explain. Why, I'll use words even your *simple* mind can comprehend.

VIVIEN. It's only you and I now and since I'm not guilty, *ta da*, you're it.

JOAN. *(pleading)* No, no, you must reconsider. You're making a terrible mistake.

VIVIEN. No, I'm not. You have guilt written all over your face.

(**JOAN** *glances into the imaginary wall mirror.*)

I could have sworn I wrote "INNOCENT."

(**VIVIEN** *grabs the poem from* **JOAN**.)

VIVIEN. Mother Paramount, since you were so insistent on killing us off according to this here poem, I feel it's my duty to read you your epitaph. Shall we? Let's.

(reading aloud)

'Two Sisters of San Andreas playing with a gun, One got herself shot, and then there was one.'

(**VIVIEN** *tosses the poem on the sofa and points the gun at* **JOAN**.)

Say your prayers, Sister.

JOAN. *(panicky)* I demand an appeal.

VIVIEN. *(snapping back)* Motion denied.

JOAN. *(intensely)* Objection. My client can't walk.

VIVIEN. Yes, you can.

JOAN. No, I can't.

VIVIEN. Can so.

JOAN. Can not.

(**VIVIEN** *stamps her feet.*)

VIVIEN. Can, can, can!

(**JOAN** *pounds on the arms of the wheelchair.*)

JOAN. Can't, can't, can't!

VIVIEN. *(screaming)* Yes, you can!

JOAN. *(screaming back)* No, I...

(to audience)

...yes I can!

(**JOAN** *leaps from the wheelchair and runs toward the bar.*)

(**VIVIEN** *fires two shots at* **JOAN** *who is 'hit.' She staggers behind the bar and, momentarily, drops out of sight.* **JOAN** *then springs back up. She is holding a white wire clothes hanger in her hand.*)

(angrily)

No, wire hangers...!

(to audience)

Well, you know.

(**JOAN** *throws the wire hanger over her shoulder. She bends over, still in pain from being shot, and pulls out a feather duster from behind the bar and frantically begins to dust the top of the bar.*)

This bar is a mess!

(to **VIVIEN***)*

Do you think it's clean? Do you think it's clean? Well, do you?

(**VIVIEN** *shoots her again.*)

(**JOAN** *turns away, grimacing. She grabs a snow globe off the bar and staggers to center stage.*)

A simple 'no' would have sufficed.

(**JOAN** *looks at the snow globe strangely, shakes it, then falls to her knees.*)

Rosebud.

(As **JOAN** *falls to the ground, the snow globe rolls out of her hand and across the floor.*)

VIVIEN. So, she *could* walk…

(catty)

…pity.

(**VIVIEN** *places the gun on the sofa, out of reach.*)

Well, I guess I've done murder.

(chipper)

But I won't think about that now…I'll think about that tomorrow.

(**VIVIEN** *reclines on the stairs and closes her eyes to rest.*)

(*The 8' tall gold statue swings open and* **GLORIA** *appears carrying Valentino.* **GLORIA** *picks up the discarded gun from the sofa and points it at* **VIVIEN**. *Sensing someone is in the room;* **VIVIEN** *opens her eyes and is startled at seeing* **GLORIA**.)

VIVIEN. *(to audience – in a loud whisper, ala "Sixth Sense")* I see dead people!

(*Throughout the following speech,* **GLORIA** *constantly talks with her hands causing the gun to waive in all directions, including toward herself. She holds Valentino in her other hand for the rest of the scene.*)

GLORIA. We Yankees never say die. My compliments. You killed Sister Joan right on schedule and according to the poem too.

(to **VIVIEN***)*

GLORIA. *(cont.)* I really know how to choose an efficient coordinator.

VIVIEN. But...you're...you're...

GLORIA. ...Dead? You have poor, gullible Sister Tallulah to thank for that. I told her we'd trap the killer by faking my death. Then I would be free to spy on the murderer. It was so easy to poison her afterwards. You all swallowed my red herring. As you can see I get very angry with those that break one of the sacred Ten Directions. So every year I invite the sinners here to Grauman's Chinese Island and this is where I kill them off...one by one. Say your prayers, Sister Vivien.

(to Valentino)

GLORIA. *(cont.)* Say goodbye, Valentino.

(to **VIVIEN***)*

'One Sister of San Andreas thinking she'd won,
A red herring deceived her, and then there was...'
none.

*(***TALLULAH** *rises from the floor.)*

VIVIEN. No, you're mad! You're mad!

*(***TALLULAH** *sneaks up, and grabs* **GLORIA** *from behind.)*

TALLULAH. Sister Vivien, grab the gun!

*(***VIVIEN** *takes the gun from a surprised* **GLORIA***.)*

VIVIEN. Good work, Sister Tallulah
(to **GLORIA***)* Thought you outfoxed us, didn't you?

*(***VIVIEN** *sticks her tongue out at* **GLORIA** *and makes a childish noise.)*

TALLULAH. All rise, Sisters. Court's in session.

(**KATHARINE** *and* **JOAN** *rise to their feet. All remaining* **SISTERS** *enter from various doors and hallways and surround* **GLORIA**.)

KATHARINE. Well, it's about bloody time. My back is killing me.

JOAN. And my butt will never be the same.

JUDY. Toto and I got tired of hanging around. Get it? Hanging around.

(**GLORIA** *snarls at* **JUDY** *who squeals and runs away.*)

HATTIE. *(to* **GLORIA***)* Shame on you, you no-account, psycho fool.

(**JOAN** *takes the gun from* **VIVIEN** *and points it at* **GLORIA**.)

JOAN. *(to* **GLORIA***)* Paramount, sit!

GLORIA. I can't believe you're still alive. You're all sinners and sinners must be punished.

(**GLORIA** *backs up to sofa and sits.* **JOAN** *sits on the other end of the sofa, still pointing the gun at* **GLORIA**.)

JOAN. And so you shall be, Mother Paramount.

GLORIA. How could I have fallen for the old "Eight-Sisters-fake-that-they're-dead-then-come-back-to-capture-Mother-Paramount" trick? How *did* you do it?

JOAN. Superb acting!

GLORIA. Brilliantly executed!

(*Simultaneously they all (except* **GLORIA***) take a quick "cast" bow.*)

ALL. *(except* **GLORIA***) (in unison)* Thank you!

MARILYN. We certainly *outmanured* you this time.

ALL. *(Correcting Marilyn, in unison)* That's *maneuvered*, Sister!

GLORIA. But how did you discover my plan?

TALLULAH. A rather hefty stool pigeon told us, dahling.

ALL. *(except* **GLORIA** *and* **MAE**) *(in unison)* Hit it, Sister Mae.

MAE. Thank you for that rather dubious introduction. You see, Mother Paramount, someone had to stop you. We knew about your plan because you slipped up last year. One of your victims was not dead. She escaped and ran to the other Sisters and told them of your wicked plan.

GLORIA. Who did I miss? Who didn't I kill?

(We hear a Harp Glissando play. **MAE** *takes off her robe revealing a full-length, pink gown. The costume is similar to Glinda's in "The Wizard of Oz."* **HATTIE** *takes a crown and wand from the bottom shelf of the table behind the sofa; puts crown on* **MAE** *and hands her the wand. The Sisters "ooh" and "aah" at the transformation. The Harp Glissando fades out.)*

MAE/GLINDA. *(Billie Burke-type voice)* It was I...Glinda, the good Sister of North 'Holywood!'

GLORIA. *(surprised)* Ah...the *popular* one! But I poisoned you last year?

MAE/GLINDA. Well, your poison wasn't very potent.

GLORIA. Damn, those generic brands!

KATHARINE. You see Mother Paramount, Sisters Vivien and Hattie engineered this entire weekend for us. The rest of us just substituted your murderer tools with harmless ones like a collapsible knife and rubber spikes *(She performs a thrust and parry movement.)* in the wall, and Sister Judy wore a neckbrace.

JUDY. And Toto Too!

GLORIA. I can't believe you all faked this. How could you? Where's your sense of religious guilt?

(now in the high-pitched witch voice)

GLORIA. *(cont.)* My plan...my beautifully wicked plan...
destroyed by you accursed brats.

*(The Sisters wince at GLORIA's voice. While JOAN
is holding her ears from the sound, GLORIA grabs
the gun from JOAN's hand. JOAN rises.)*

Stand back, all of you, or I'll let you have it.

JOAN. I hate to disillusion you, Mother Paramount; but
there's only one bullet left in that gun and once
you've...*killed Bette*...

(All Sisters quickly take one step away from BETTE.)

*(JOAN repeatedly nods her head toward BETTE as
she leans out of the line of fire.)*

...the rest of us will get you.

GLORIA. You have a point there.

*(GLORIA grabs her own throat and points the gun
to her own stomach!)*

(ala Peter Lorre)

One more step and Paramount takes a powder.

*(They all look at JOAN. JOAN shrugs "yes." All take
one step towards GLORIA.)*

I warned you!

(GLORIA shoots herself and falls to her knees.)

JUDY. She didn't?!

KATHARINE. She did.

ALL. *(In unison. Sarcastically)* Pity.

GLORIA. *(still ala Peter Lorre)* Look what you made me
do to my dress.

(gasping in her normal voice)

Now you've got me mad. I'm a human being, damn
it! My life had value. It can't end this way. I have
to get up now. In fact, I want all of you to get up;

drag your bleeding bodies to the window; open it, stick out your head and yell, 'I'm mad as hell and I'm not going to take Joan Crawford's overacting any more!'

(**GLORIA** *gasps and looks at* **JOAN**.)

GLORIA. *(cont.)* Sister Joan, I think I'm really seeing you for the first time in my life and you're cheap and horrible...and those are your good qualities.

(**GLORIA** *gasps and crosses to* **JUDY**, **MARILYN** *and* **BETTE**.)

(ala Judy Garland)

I had a dream...

(to **JUDY***)*

and you were there,

(to **MARILYN***)*

and you, and

(to **BETTE***)*

My God, it was a nightmare.

(**GLORIA** *gasps and mimics* **BETTE**.)

Sister Bette, let's not ask for the stars when we have the moon. I'm the star...

(**GLORIA** *turns around and "moons"* **BETTE**.)

...and here's the moon.

(All gasp.)

(**GLORIA** *falls to her knees and reaches her arms up to the sky.)*

GLORIA. *(cont.)* Cancel my close-up, Sister DeMille.

(**GLORIA** *falls motionless to the floor, still clutching Valentino. All the other Sisters applaud.)*

TALLULAH. Talk about cliche' deaths, dahlings.

JUDY. She's dead Toto...dead. And you're all here. And this is my room. And I'm not going to leave here ever, ever again, because I love you all...and...oh, Auntie Em!

ALL. *(in unison)* Oh, shut up!

KATHARINE. This calls for a celebration. I never thought I'd be the one to say this, but Sister Tallulah...line 'em up.

TALLULAH. My pleasure, dahlings. I've been saving a bottle for such an occasion.

*(**TALLULAH** brings out an opened bottle of wine and a tray with nine glasses from the bottom shelf of the bar. They all gather around the bar. **TALLULAH** begins to pour the wine.)*

KATHARINE. Is it something special?

TALLULAH. It's Chateau Chevalier, 1942.

(The Sisters pass the glasses around until they all have one.)

KATHARINE. You know, Sisters. I think this is the beginning of a beautiful friendship. L'chaim.

(They all raise their glasses.)

ALL. *(in unison)* To life!

(They all drink their wine and place their glasses on the bar in unison. After two beats a startled look appears on all their faces.)

ALL. *(in unison)* Uh, oh.

*(They all collapse dead around the bar. There is a slight pause, and then Valentino rises, looks around room, making sure the "coast is clear." Valentino taps **GLORIA** on the shoulder with his beak. **GLORIA** sits up. She then rises to her feet.)*

GLORIA. Obviously, 1942 was not a very good year for Chateau Chevalier...

(pause)

...pity. Did these sinners really think they outwitted me? What fools, 'eh Valentino?

(directly to Valentino)

What's that? Of course they're all dead; I poisoned the wine myself. I knew they'd drink a toast of the finest wine to our defeat.

(listens to Valentino a moment)

Come again. Yes, they *did* fall for the old 'Eight-Sisters-fake-that-they're-dead-come-back-to-capture-Mother-Paramount-who-knew-of-their-plan-then-double-crossed-them-at-their-own-game' trick.

(listens again)

Yes Valentino, as a matter of fact I have chosen next years ten victims.

(listens again)

Yes. That *Angelina Jolie* has been a real pain in the ass...but she won't be for long.

(GLORIA *laughs and ascends the stairs to the balcony as the* **gong doorbell** *is heard.)*

Who can that be? I've poisoned them all.

(SISTER ALFRED *enters the room pointing a gun at* **GLORIA** *who backs away.)*

ALFRED. Good evening, my pretty.

GLORIA. What are you doing here?

ALFRED. I've come to prevent you from returning next year to commit what is considered the ultimate sin in Holywood.

GLORIA. What's that?

ALFRED. The "sequel."

(**ALFRED** *shoots* **GLORIA.** *She dramatically rolls down the main stairs to the living room floor, dead.*)

(*to* **GLORIA,** *ala "The Apprentice"*) "You're fired!'

(*to audience*)

Th-th-th-th-that's all, folks.

(*Playoff* **LET'S SAY, "HOORAY FOR HOLY-WOOD"** *Reprise for curtain call.*)

(*Blackout*)

(*Curtain*)

The End

PROPERTY/SET DRESSING PLOT

Prop Name	Character
Hollywood Map with removable "L" & Caricature	(Stage Crew)
Pointer	Sister Alfred

Onstage	Character
Loveseat Sofa (with (2) throw pillows)	(Set Dressing/ Mae)
Sofa Table (behind sofa with (2) shelves)	(Set Dressing)
Bar	(Set Dressing)
(3) Barstools	(Set Dressing)
Corner shelf (behind bar with (5) shelves)	(Set Dressing)
Picture Window (with drapes that can be opened & closed)	(Set Dressing)
8' Gold Statue (with hidden passageway)	(Set Dressing)
Small Side Table (for Coffee Service)	(Set Dressing)
Balcony (with black & white checkered tile floor)	(Set Dressing)
Victrola with Record	(Set Dressing)
Palm Tree & Pot with sand	(Set Dressing)

Front Entranceway	Character
iPod (mounted on wall by pillars)	(Set Dressing)
Vase with Flowers (on pedestal)	(Set Dressing)
Pedestal	(Set Dressing)

Walls & Stage Area	Character
Light Switches (by all doorways)	(Set Dressing)
Portrait of Mother Paramount (hinged to wall above 6" China Nuns)	(Set Dressing)
(10) 6" China Nuns on a Silver Tray (on pedestal)	(Set Dressing)
Pedestal	(Set Dressing)
Small Gold Statue (on shelf by closet)	Bette

Closet	Character
Curtain & white Curtain Rod	(Set Dressing)
Clothes Rod (inside closet)	(Set Dressing)
WWI Army Helmet	Gloria
Broom	Gloria
Bare Light Bulb w/Pull Cord (or chain)	(Set Dressing)
Shower Curtain	Hattie
Garment Bag (with hole cut in bottom)	Gloria

Window	Character
Full length Drapes/Curtains (must be opened and closed)	(Set Dressing)
Large Tree (outside window with (1) horizontal limb)	(Set Dressing)
(2) Hangman's Noose	Judy/Toto

Coffee Service (on side table)	Character
Silver Coffee Pot	(Set Dressing)
Silver Serving Tray	(Set Dressing)
(2) Candle Holders with Candles	(Set Dressing)
(4) Coffee Cups ((2) white & (2) black)	Joan

Sofa & Sofa Table (w/2 shelves)	Character
Ash Tray with Lighter	(Set Dressing)
Rose with Vase	(Set Dressing)
(2) Flashlights (bottom shelf)	Hattie
Fake Moustache (preset in sofa)	Gloria
Baby Powder (bottom shelf)	Gloria
Pen	Gloria
Box of Chocolates	Bette
Screwdriver (preset in sofa – large with white handle)	Joan
Telephone	Marilyn
Book ("Swingin' With Swanson" Biography)	Gloria
Book ("Boozin' With Tallulah" Biography)	Tallulah
Bouquet of Cala Lilies	Katharine
Glinda Hat & Wand (bottom shelf)	Hattie/Mae

Bar	Character
Pack of Cigarettes (top shelf)	Tallulah
Cigarette Lighter (refillable) (top of bar)	Tallulah
Ash Tray (top of bar)	Tallulah
(6) Bar Glasses (top shelf)	Tallulah
Extra Rag (for spills) (bottom shelf)	Tallulah
Bottle of Pepsi (sealed) (top shelf)	Tallulah/Joan
Garden Trowel (top shelf)	Tallulah
Green Visor (bottom shelf)	Katharine
Deck of Cards	Katharine
Bottle of Vodka (bottom shelf)	Tallulah
(2) Numbered Flash Cards (5.2) (top shelf)	Tallulah
(2) Numbered Flash Cards (0.0) (top shelf)	Bette
(2) Cigarette Lighters (disposable) (top shelf)	Tallulah/ Katharine
(2) Wire Clothes Hangers – white (bottom shelf)	Joan
Snow Globe (bottom shelf)	Joan
Wine Bottle (bottom shelf)	Tallulah
Tray with (9) Bar Glasses (bottom shelf)	Tallulah

Corner Shelf (behind Bar)	Character
Framed Poem ("Ten Sisters of San Andreas")	Tallulah

Stage Right Props	Character
Pointer	Alfred
Feather Duster	Hattie
Jeweled Mirror Ring	Vivien
Fan	Vivien
Sunglasses	Bette
Sunglasses	Joan
Wheelchair (with practical Buzzer)	Joan
(2) Suitcases: (1) black & (1) white	Bette
Birdcage with Fake Bird on Perch	Bette
Spotted Gloves (white with black spots)	Bette
Sunglasses	Tallulah

Sunglasses	Gloria
(1) Large Suitcase (black)	Gloria
Portable Bar (with "BAR" prominently printed on the side)	Tallulah
– with (3) liquor decanters – vodka, gin & bourbon	
Sunglasses	Katharine
Sunglasses	Mae
(1) Carpet Bag Suitcase	Katharine
(1) Large Suitcase (black) (with "M" monogram painted on side)	Mae
Extremely Oversized Feather Hat	Mae
Feather Boa (white & black)	Mae
Sunglasses	Judy
Basket (white) with large Pill Bottle with Pills	Judy
Toto (mechanical dog that barks w/collar, leash & sunglasses)	Judy
Sunglasses	Marilyn
Purse (white) (with reading glasses)	Marilyn
(1) Vanity Case	Marilyn
Chef's Hat (white)	Gloria
Hors d'oeuvre Tray (with fake sliced salami and cheese on crackers)	Gloria
Oversized Meat Cleaver (fake)	Gloria
Furniture Dolly with (4) Casters and Long Pull Rope	Hattie/Gloria
Loaf of Bread (fake)	Gloria
White Dusting Cloth	Gloria
Bag of Leaves	(Stage Crew)
Blue & White Checkered Dress and Hair Ribbons (for quick-change)	Judy
Blue Bobby Socks (for quick-change)	Judy
Red Ruby Slippers (for quick-change)	Judy
Pink Lawn Flamingo ("Valentino") with Sheik's Desert Headdress	Gloria
Red Rose	Gloria
Watch	Hattie
Gun ("Yankee Killer")	Vivien
Leg Holster (for "Yankee Killer")	Hattie
(10) Large Feather Fans (white)	(Cast)
Black Glove	(Stage Crew)
Lampshade with Fringe	Katharine
(2) 12" Tent Spikes	Katharine
Hangman's Noose	Tallulah
Oversized Kitchen Knife (fake)	Marilyn
Gunshot	(Stage Crew)
Baby Bette Doll (with cigarette in her hand)	Bette
(2) Swanson Frozen TV Dinners	Bette
Bunch of Grapes (fake)	Bette
Serving Tray (black)	Bette
– Shredded Wheat ("tweet") Box with Blue Feathers	
– Cereal Bowl (white)	
8" x 10" Picture of Joan (for bottom of Bird Cage)	Bette

Blue Feather Duster (missing some feathers)	Bette
Red Herring (stuffed) (preset in Gloria's coat)	Gloria
Stage Left Props	**Character**
Baseball Bat	Hattie
"The Daily Variety"	Bette
Cigarette	Bette
(10) Large Feather Fans (white)	(Cast)
"Paramount" Mountain Cut-Out (dance number)	Joan
Vial of Liquid	Mae
Small Gold Statue	Bette
Scissors (large)	Vivien
Book ("Mae West On Sex" Biography)	Mae
(2) Balloons (Mae's breasts)	Mae
Push Pin (hidden between Mae's fingers to "pop" balloons)	Mae
(2) Kneepads	Mae
Mop	Hattie
Small Silver Tray with (3) Votive Candles	Joan
(6) Numbered Flash Cards (5.3, 5.4, 5.6)	Vivien/ Katharine/ Hattie
American Flag Underskirt (for Gloria's quick-change)	Gloria
(1) Cigarette Lighter (disposable)	Vivien
(2) Knee Pads	Joan
(2) Knee Pads	Gloria
Gun	Alfred
Miscellaneous Description	**Character**
Cigarettes, Cigarette Case, finger-held Cigarette Holder, Lighter, portable Ashtray	Gloria
Mirror with Joan's likeness, Toothbrush, Bon Ami	Joan
(2) Numbered Flash Cards (5.0)	
Cigarettes, Lighter	Bette
Eyeglasses	Marilyn

COSTUME PLOT

Character	Costume
Alfred	Black Suit (pants & jacket)
	White long-sleeve Shirt
	Black Tie (thin)
	Black Shoes
	Black Wimple with White Collar
Hattie	White Chef's Shirt
	Black Skirt (long)
	White Apron (long)
	Red Petticoat (long)
	Black Shoes
	Black/White Bandana
	Black Wimple with White Collar
Vivien	White Hoop Dress with Large Black Tassles
	Hoop Skirt
	Pantaloons
	Black Shoes
	Black Wig (or ringlets)
	Black Wimple with White Collar
Joan	Black Dress (with padded shoulders)
	Black Spike Shoes (with ankle straps)
	40's style Black Wig
	Black Wimple with White Collar
Bette	White Dress with Black Bow (in back)
	Black/White Striped Tights
	Black Mary Jane Shoes
	Black/White Spotted ("Dalmation") Gloves
	Bathrobe
	Slippers
	Hair Curlers
	Blonde Curly Wig
	Black Wimple with White Collar
Gloria	Black Skirt (long)
	White Blouse
	Black Shoes
	Black Overcoat
	American Flag Underskirt
	Black/White Turban
	20's Style Spit Curl (on forehead)
	Black Wimple with White Collar

Tallulah	Black Tea-Length Cocktail Dress
	Black Shoes
	Rhinestone Necklace/Bracelet
	Long Auburn Wavy Wig
	Black Wimple with White Collar
Katharine	Black Pants
	Black (or White) Turtleneck Shirt
	Black Shirt (long, oversized)
	White Keds Tennis Shoes
	Wrap (velvet) Jacket/Coat
	Black Wimple with White Collar
Mae	Black Beaded Dress
	Black/White Feathered Boa
	Black High-Heel Shoes
	Oversized Hat with Large Feathers
	Rhinestone Necklace/Bracelets/Rings
	White Nightgown
	Black Bathrobe (slinky)
	Slippers
	"Glinda" Pink Dress
	"Glinda" Pink Hat
	"Glinda" Pink Shoes
	"Glinda" Wig
	Blonde Curly Wig (short)
	Black Wimple with White Collar
Judy	Black/White Checkered Dress
	Black/White Hair Bows
	White Bobby Socks
	Black Shoes
	Blue/White Checkered Dress
	Blue/White Hair Bows
	Blue Bobby Socks
	Red Ruby Slippers
	Auburn Wig (with 2 braids)
	Black Wimple with White Collar
Marilyn	White Pleated Halter Dress
	Black/White High-Heel Shoes
	Rhinestone Necklace/Bracelets
	Blonde Wig
	Black Wimple with White Collar

Let's Say "Hooray for Holywood"!

from the play "And Then There Was Nun"

Words and Music
by
Craig Victor Fenter

LEAD SHEET

Let's say "Hoo - ray for Ho - ly - wood where a cam" - ra turns your gran - ma in - to Do - ris Day. Come, join our or - der and you can be a star in just one day, in Ho - ly - wood. Hoo - ray! O - pen - ing night is a fab - u - lous sight, e - spe - ci'ly if you're in "the know". But, bet - ter be - ware of that girl with red hair; she'd kill to be in the next

back - ers all tell them, "Let's go"! Let's say "Hoo - ray, Hoo -

[shouted, not sung!]

ray, Hoo - ray for Ho - ly wood!" where it's

tren - dy to be friend - ly 'til you get your way. Come,

join our or - der and you can be a star in just one day, in Ho - ly - wood.

Hoo - ray! [Optional cut-off before F#]

"... AND THERE WAS NUN"

Written by: Bruce W. Gilray & Richard T. Witter
PV Players, Torrance, CA
April, 1996

Set Design by: Susan A. Lyan
Construction Foreman: Gary Krenz

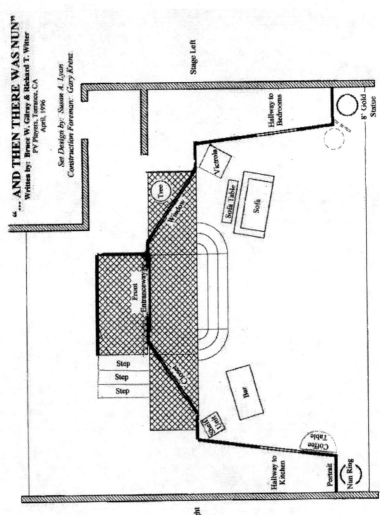

OTHER TITLES AVAILABLE FROM SAMUEL FRENCH

JUDY'S SCARY LITTLE CHRISTMAS

Book by David Church and Jim Webber
Music and Lyrics by Joe Patrick Ward

Holiday Musical Comedy / 7m, 6f / Simple Set

Judy Garland is primed for her biggest comeback ever - the dazzling star of her own TV special, broadcast live on Christmas Eve, 1959. Judy's guests include Bing Crosby (making some holiday "grog"), Ethel Merman (plugging her Hawaiian album), and Liberace (with a handsome sailor in tow). However, mysterious snafus behind the scenes and cameo appearances by commie-baiting Vice President Richard Nixon (who performs a magic act) and blacklisted writer, Lillian Hellman, (who's forced to read "Children's Letter to Santa" with a puppet) throw Judy's program off course. The surprises climax when the arrival of Joan Crawford is interrupted by the spectral figure of…Death. The evening takes a detour into the twilight zone as the celebrities are forced to confront the lies behind their legends. Devastated and alone, Judy meets a special fan who ultimately proves that, despite her flaws, her shining legacy still endures.

"Magical! A side-splitting musical parody…wickedly funny!"
– *Los Angeles Times*

"Wonderfully strange…a true holiday treat!"
– *Hollywood Reporter*

"A non-stop hoot!"
– *Back Stage West*

"Hilarious! A surreal snow globe highball; a Hollywood Christmas card from beyond the grave!"
– *Portland Mercury*

OTHER TITLES AVAILABLE FROM SAMUEL FRENCH

KARLABOY

Steven Peros

Drama / 6m, 2f

* WINNER *
1994 Drama-Logue Critics Award Outstanding Achievement in Writing

Biographer Bill Lauder has penned a ruthless tell-all about Karla Daven, a long dead legendary 1950's starlet. As a result, he is summoned in the middle of the night to the dilapidated mansion of Karla's celebrity husband, Harold Bachman, a reclusive director who makes the outlandish claim that Karla's ghost has threatened to kill him this very night unless Bill calls off the publication of his tawdry book of lies.

What follows is an intense evening where memory wrestles with myth in order to find the truth. As Harold gets deeper into exposing Bill's lies about Karla, he is forced to confront the lies he's told himself – lies about himself as a filmmaker, a husband, and as a man. Harold must not only save himself from Karla's ghost, but from the ghosts of an unrealized life.

"Steven Peros' intriguing play is a well wrought tale of love and loss, set against the sweeping background of the golden era of Hollywood … while the characters are fictional, they take on a life of their own and end up eerily reminiscent and real … *Karlaboy* could rightly take its place among the more innovative and involving productions currently on the Los Angeles theatre scene."
- Elias Stimac, *Drama-Logue*

"A wonderful experience … what rings through this totally fascinating play is the brilliant dialogue. Steven Peros has an ear for dialogue of this type – highly intelligent, witty and on the mark. You'll see many a show before you come across talk this stimulating."
- Maurice Keller, *The Tolucan*

OTHER TITLES AVAILABLE FROM SAMUEL FRENCH

A HISTORY OF AMERICAN FILM

Newly revised!

Book and Lyrics by Christopher Durang
Score by Mel Marvin

Full Length, Musical / 9m, 6f / Various sets

A hilarious take off on American films, especially from the 1930s through the 1950s. The principals play a variety of characters. There is a Cagney/Bogart/Dean/Brando type-and a Fonda/Stewart/ Peck/ Perkins type. The women, too, are types-basically Bette Davis, Loretta Young and Eve Arden. The parts they play are wild parodies from many Hollywood genres; a silent tearjerker, slum idyll, gangster epic, court-room melodrama, chain gang social justice thriller, screwball comedy, Busby Berkeley backstage musical, war propaganda canteen musical-not to forget "*Casablanca*," "*Citizen Kane*" and a variety of minor genres.

"The special gifts Durang brings to this work, apart from a sharp eye for genre parody are a sense of the misguided way we watch movies-making stars, ignoring the character in favor of the actor, wallowing in the kitschier moments-and an equally lethal sense of how Hollywood played on our sentimentalities by using the actor and the kitsch forms to put junky ideas across."
- *Village Voice*

"Authentic, inspired and possessed comedy...A very funny carnival."
- *The New York Times*